To David
and
to Mount Rainier, Maryland

Until one has loved an animal, a part of one's
soul remains unawakened.
— Anatole France

CONTENTS

Oswald

THE ALMOST FAMOUS OPOSSUM

Written by
Sara Pascoe

Illustrated by
Varya Kolesnikova

TRINDLES & GREEN

www.sarapascoe.co/info@sarapascoe.co/

ISBN: 978-0-9935747-0-2

Published by Trindles and Green, Ltd
Loxwood, 6 Alumdale Road
Bournemouth, BH4 8HX
United Kingdom
www.trindlesandgreen.com

Distributed by Atlasbooks (1-800-BOOK LOG or 1-800-266-5564)

Varya Kolesnikova, Illustrator. behance.net/paskamarja
Lindsey Alexander, Editor. http://www.lindsey-alexander.com
Anton Nesterov, front cover design. behance.net/antonnesterov

1

OSWALD'S ENDEAVORS

Joey tried to remember what his mom had just said. She stood there with her arms crossed and her brow furrowed. Her curly hair shone in the kitchen lights, bright compared to the dimming sky outside this May evening. The counters were spotless, although you could still smell the macaroni, cheese, and broccoli casserole they'd had for dinner. Some of Joey's excellent test results were displayed on the refrigerator, much to Joey's embarrassment. Not that there was really anyone to be embarrassed in front of these days. He risked glimpsing through the glass doors to the back deck. Oswald, his good opossum friend, blinked back and shifted from foot to foot to foot to foot.

"Come on, we've got to get going," Melvin, Joey's cat, said from the floor next to the door.

"I know," Joey answered.

"You know what?" his mother, Ann, asked.

"Uh oh," Melvin said and swooshed out the cat flap.

Ann tipped Joey's face up to hers. He looked away—everyone said his almond-shaped brown eyes gave away what he was thinking. "You were talking to the cat, weren't you?" She shook her head, but didn't wait for an answer. "Bread. You were going to go get some more so I can make your sandwiches for tomorrow. Remember?"

Joey smiled as he grabbed his bicycle helmet. "Of course I remember," he said and bounded out the door.

"What took you so long?" Oswald felt as cross as Ann had looked. But he never could stay annoyed with the boy for long. He was such a lovely lad, always interested in new things and up for adventure. *Yes, becoming quite a nice young fellow, under my guidance,* he thought.

"Hey, we had to eat all the bread while his mom wasn't looking so he had an excuse to go out on a school night. Don't get your tail in a knot," Melvin huffed, as he maneuvered between the boy and opossum.

"My tail is prehensile, but I certainly don't tie it in knots," Oswald said proudly.

Melvin narrowed his eyes. "Glad we have *that* straightened out."

"OK, you guys. Ready?" Joey said, as he plunked his bicycle helmet over his dark curls and continued before he got an answer. "I'll go get my bike." He leaped down the stairs and disappeared behind the garage.

Oswald was nervous, winding and unwinding his tail around his front leg.

"You'll be all right. We've been over this a thousand times," Melvin said.

"I think it was more like twelve. There's no need for *hyperbole.*" Oswald paused to see if Melvin understood this big word. Oswald was going to be famous, and fame, he knew, came with responsibilities, like setting a good example for others, being a role model. Improving his vocabulary was one of the ways he'd been preparing for his new life.

Joey glided his bike to a stop beside the deck.

"Whatever, man," Melvin said and jumped into the large basket on the front. He settled in on an old towel nestled atop a large coil of rope in the basket. Joey clipped his chinstrap in place, grabbed the handlebars, and put a foot on a pedal.

"Come on, Oswald. Let's go," Joey said.

Oswald peered over the edge of the deck. It was a full four feet to the ground, and exactly eleven inches from the deck to the bicycle basket. Joey had measured it for him—twice. Oswald had jumped farther than that lots of times, when climbing down trees, for example. But now, as the sun was starting to set, and his best friends were ready to help him make his dreams come true, those inches telescoped out in front of him. *What if something goes wrong? What if I don't get into the newspaper?* Becoming famous had been Oswald's dream for so long he didn't know what he'd do without it. His mother always told him he would "be a real somebody, be important someday." And now that she was gone, he wanted to prove her right all the more.

Boy and cat stared at him. It wouldn't do to discuss his trepidation now; it certainly wasn't full-blown fear.

"Do you think that old towel is suitable? Might you have something nicer?" Oswald said.

All at once, Melvin jumped back onto the deck and shoved Oswald over the edge. Joey caught him and carefully lifted him into the basket.

Melvin leapt back in and Joey clipped a bungee cord across the basket as a sort of seat belt, just as his mother opened the back door.

"Joey? Oh good, you're still here."

"Dang." Melvin shoved Oswald underneath him and Joey tugged the towel over them, leaving only Melvin's head sticking out. Ann walked down the steps and handed Joey some money.

"Looks like we're out of peanut butter, too. Can you please get a jar while you're at it?"

"Sure, Mom."

"You better be growing—you're eating me out of house and home." She looked down at the bicycle basket. "You sure it's a good idea to take poor Melvin? Wouldn't he rather stay here?" She reached for the cat, but Joey banged his foot on the pedal and started across the yard.

"Nah, he likes to ride," Joey called over his shoulder.

Joey sped through the front gate and onto the quiet street. Melvin shrugged the towel off, and Oswald gasped for air.

"Was that necessary?" Oswald sputtered.

Joey had taken Oswald on a couple of short rides before, up and down the block to get him used to it, but now it felt like they were flying. The tires thrummed as Joey stood to go even faster. Oswald thought he might be sick. He looked at Melvin, whiskers and ears blown back, a look of bliss on his furry face.

"Isn't this great? It's because of you we got this ride, man. Thanks," Melvin said.

Oswald could tell Joey, too, was in the zone; boy and bicycle were one seamless machine. They had been so helpful with Oswald's endeavors. *They should have their fun, too,* he reasoned. He turned forward, gripped the basket, and closed his eyes.

2

THE CLIMB

"Hey, we're here. Get a move on." Melvin nudged Oswald and sprung out of the basket. Oswald opened one eye, then the other. He'd been so intent on not fainting from fear—this would have been a terrible time for it—that he hadn't noticed the bicycle had stopped. Joey crouched down and fastened one end of the long rope around Melvin's middle with a climbing clip, like a very long leash. The cat and boy walked over to the large oak tree at the back of the library. The remaining coils of rope hung over Joey's shoulder like he was some kind of rodeo star.

Melvin jumped onto the trunk and stuck like Velcro before climbing straight up. Joey unfurled the rope behind the cat, glancing at the bike.

"Come on, Oswald."

"Oh, yes, of course. Indubitably." Oswald climbed out of the basket and scurried over to the thick base of the tree. Strong branches reached out on all sides. One branch made a rasping sound as it scraped against the library roof in a breeze that didn't reach the ground. The leaves blocked all but a few slashes of dusk with a sliver of moon peeking over the library roof.

"Oh dear, I think we forgot my harness. I'm ever so sorry about this, Joey, but I think we'll have to try this again another night," Oswald said.

"No problemo." Joey pulled a red nylon harness from his back pocket and tossed it to Oswald.

"Look, Oswald," Melvin said from halfway up the tree, "if you don't want to do this, tell us now and we can all go home."

"What? No. Of course I want to go ahead. If all those other animals can get into the newspaper, and for such silly things like getting locked in a store overnight, or riding on a bus, well then, I think it's *my* turn. Don't you think so?" Oswald paused and looked at his two friends. They nodded their agreement.

He stepped into the harness and waddled over to Joey, who clipped it together. Oswald started up, spiraling round and round the large tree trunk.

"Oh brother, this is going to take a while," Melvin said, watching from above. The cat shook his head, then stepped from the branch onto the roof. He took a few steps to a small round window, tilted open to let hot air out.

After what seemed like a very long time, Oswald arrived on the branch that reached the roof. Oswald clung on as it bowed with his weight.

"Well, come on already." Melvin was washing his face with his paw. "We don't have forever. His mom thinks he's gone to get a loaf of bread and peanut butter."

"I know. I was there," Oswald said.

"Yeah, and it was hard work eating it all *after* dinner," Joey called from below.

"Shh," Melvin said. "Don't blow our cover."

"Oh, right, sorry. Oswald, unclip the rope from Melvin, then clip it onto your harness. Melvin, help him," Joey whisper-shouted through cupped hands.

"If he'd get off the stupid branch," Melvin said, then grabbed Oswald's harness with his teeth and tugged, pulling Oswald onto the roof. Oswald grunted fear and surprise.

"Don't forget this was *your* idea, Oswald," Melvin said.

Despite some fussing, they managed to unclip the rope from Melvin and clipped it onto Oswald's harness.

"Oswald's ready to be lowered in," Melvin called down to Joey.

"I am?" Oswald said. "Are you sure this clip can hold my weight? Maybe we should test it."

"We did already, a kazillion times, remember?" Melvin said, eyes narrowed. It was all Oswald could do not to point out his poor word choice.

"Oswald, relax," Joey called out. "The clip can hold up to—"

"Stop right there." A flashlight beam swirled through the tree, then rested on Joey. A tired-looking man in a navy-blue security uniform looked hard at the boy. "Drop whatever's in your hands and put them above your head where I can see them."

Joey dropped the rope and stomped on it. Oswald gasped as he plummeted then jolted to a stop swinging in small circles above the library floor a long way below.

"It's the heat, man," Melvin called to Oswald through the window. "Got to go."

The rope rasped through the tree again and over the window ledge. Joey must have let out more rope accidentally. Oswald lurched again, this time far enough so that he was level with the second floor. It made a ring around the open atrium in the center. Oswald looked down and gulped. The floor was a good fifteen feet below. But that wasn't Oswald's only worry. *Police of some sort, oh dear. I hope Joey remembers to be extra polite and not talk back.* Oswald strained to hear what was going on outside.

"I'm sorry, sir. It's just me and my cat. We don't mean any harm—"

"Step away from the tree where I can see you, and keep your hands up!"

Joey had no choice but to step off the rope. He heard a faint swoosh, then something between a clunk and a smack. Poor Oswald must have landed in the library, but not as they'd planned. Joey hoped he was all right. He flinched as he imagined the rest of the rope coiling on top of the likely not very pleased possum. He couldn't help but look up and the security guard followed his gaze. Luckily Melvin was scrambling down the tree.

"What's going on up there?" the security guard asked.

"Meow!" Melvin meowed his cutest—no doubt attempting to win over the security guard.

"You see," Joey say, trying his best to think faster than he spoke, "That's my cat, Melvin. He made Cat Climbing Champ of Mount Rainier two years in a row and got third place in Prince George's County last year. We're training for the state try-outs next month, and this tree here, well, it's one of the tallest and best climbing trees around."

"Hold up now, son—slow down," the guard said. "You mean to tell me you came here *with* your cat, so he can practice climbing?"

"Yes, sir."

"And how old are you?"

"Ten, sir. Ten and two months." He rattled off his full date of birth.

"You're tall for ten."

"Yes, sir, everybody says so."

"Does your mother know you're out here?"

"Oh, no. My mom sent me out to get bread and peanut butter, but I forgot all about it, and now I'm gonna be—"

"Well, you best be going, then."

Melvin leaped into the bike basket with a small thump as Joey flung himself onto his bike and jumped on the pedals.

"Hey, don't forget your helmet," the security guard said.

"Yes, sir, thank you," Joey said, his voice fading as he raced into the night.

3

HIGH-MAINTENANCE MARSUPIAL

From the cool, smooth library table where Oswald had landed, he blinked up at the small dark window in the ceiling. It looked so far away from this distance. He smelled musty paper and new carpet. He climbed out of the pile of rope. He used his back paw, with its handy opposable big toe, like a thumb, to try to unclip himself from the harness. He could feel the clip, but couldn't open it. He grunted and tried with the other back paw, but that was no better. After rolling around a few times, all he managed to do was roll onto a chair and then plunk to the floor.

Surrounded by tall shelves stacked with books and newspapers, he was momentarily distracted from his rope problems. "Yes, yes. I need a book, a serious book. Then, I can be reading it when the staff come in tomorrow morning," he said aloud, being in the habit of talking to himself when he was alone. He smiled as he imagined his photo in the *Washington Post*'s Animal Watch column, sitting in the library reading. Perhaps he'd be interviewed on TV. Maybe asked to sign autographs. Yes, this would show he was different from the other animals who got into the newspaper for trivial things. This would certainly launch his career—who knows where it might lead?

He started walking the length of the library, hoping this would untangle the rope while he searched for the right book. "This one looks good—lots of big words in the title." He tugged it from the shelf with his teeth, then pushed it along the floor, back toward the table he had landed on. But then he noticed a small purple object under another table and left the book on the floor to investigate. It was just a hair clip, but it could come in handy, so he carried it in his tail and headed back to the book. But he took a few wrong turns, then a few more; when he came to the end of his rope, he was no closer to the book or where he started. Visions of fame popped like soap bubbles on a hot afternoon. He sat on his haunches and drummed his fingers on his sternum while he looked around for an idea. There it was—another excellent book, this one had a picture of lasagna on the cover, his favorite.

Yes, I could tell them I'm planning to open my own restaurant. Oswald thought about being the first animal to run a restaurant and how it would have a special section for animal customers. *Ah, two more firsts! Yes, there will be no stopping me.* Thoughts about everything he would do once he was famous spun in his head through the night until he heard keys jangle in the door and footsteps.

Wonderful, splendid, marvelous—this is IT! Oswald sat up and smoothed his face fur. He heard a woman singing to herself, and somewhere doors opened and closed. The overhead lights came on. Oswald saw her legs as she bustled around, straightening chairs, picking up stray bits of paper.

Suddenly, she froze.

She crouched down and blinked at Oswald.

"What in tarnation?" She looked around, followed the tangle of rope with her eyes, extended a hand toward Oswald, then retracted it.

"Ah, good morning. Let me introduce myself. I'm Oswald, the opossum of Perry Street, and I've come here to do research for my new restaurant."

"Oh, dear. I'm afraid I don't speak Animal. Are you hurt? How did you get in here?" the librarian said before she was able to stop herself from speaking, realizing she wouldn't be able to understand even if the possum did answer her. She shook her head and stood up. "I'll call Animal Control. Even if I open the door, you're all tangled up—best to have someone make sure you're not hurt."

She hurried away, leaving Oswald on his own. He could hear her on the phone: "Yes, thank you. If you could please send someone right away, before we open, that would be much appreciated."

She returned to Oswald and placed a bowl of water and a granola bar broken in pieces on a paper towel down in front of him. "I looked it up, you're an omnivore. Thought this would tide you over. Don't want you getting dehydrated on me," she said and walked away.

"Thank you—very kind," Oswald said, forgetting she didn't understand Animal.

About a half hour later, there was a knock at the door. "I'm here for a possum problem," a man said. Oswald recognized the voice—Darnell Anderson, Prince George's County Animal Control officer.

"Good morning, Darnell!" Oswald called out.

"Is he distressed?" the librarian said, hearing Oswald's sounds.

"Oh, Oswald—what have you done now?" Darnell called out then turned to the librarian. "No, trust me—he's fine. But wait 'til I get a hold of him," Darnell said.

The librarian gave a nervous laugh.

"Don't worry—I'm just playing." He pulled a microchip scanner from his pocket and waved it. "If it's him, we go way back," Darnell said.

"Oh." She laughed again. "Should I show you where he is?"

"That's OK," he said, looking under the tables. "I see him."

A few minutes later, Oswald was in the transport cage on the front seat next to Darnell as he drove the van away. He unlatched the cage lid with one hand as he pulled onto Rhode Island Avenue and headed east. Oswald popped up, leaning against the edge of the cage.

"Did you see what I was reading? Don't forget to put that in your report. It's perfect for the weekly newspaper report."

"Yeah, perfect."

There was a moment of quiet between them. The van rumbled down the road.

"Might you have any donuts, Darnell?"

Darnell didn't answer but drove on.

"Any lemon custard by chance?" Oswald persisted.

Darnell shook his head as he made a turn. "You are one high-maintenance marsupial. You do realize we have *real* animal problems to deal with. Animals in all sorts of bad situations. You're being selfish with all this nonsense—ever think of that?" Darnell stopped the van at the side of the road. There was a patch of woods with no houses. "This is your stop."

"Yes, yes. Of course, I understand, you must go by regulations. And I do appreciate it, this isn't too far from home."

Darnell clipped the cage shut and swung it out of the van. "You know, you're building quite a record as a nuisance animal. I'd stop now if I were you."

"I understand, I really do. You will write this up for your reports, won't you?"

"Of course." Darnell placed the cage on the grass, opened the side panel, and made a sweeping gesture. "Show time."

When Oswald didn't budge, Darnell gently shook him out of the cage and went back to the van.

"Good to see you. Thanks again. Try to remember to spell my name correctly, *Oswald* with an 's,'" Oswald said to Darnell's back.

Darnell glanced over his shoulder, then hopped in the van and drove off.

Oswald sniffed the air, looked for the position of the sun, and waddled off toward home. "Splendid, marvelous. I'm sure to make the news."

4

POSSUM PROVERBS

It took Oswald the rest of the day and most of the next to walk home. He got lost a few times, but reassured himself with the old possum proverb, "A possum lost is a possum who doesn't know where he is." Along the route, he found two slices of pizza with the perfect amount of mold on them—delicious.

It was Wednesday evening when he got home: the day the Animal Watch column came out in the newspaper. He couldn't wait to see himself in print: "Possum Proves Marsupial Minds are Magnificent," or maybe, "Brilliant Opossum Discovered in Library." He vibrated with excitement.

He squeezed under the front gate, climbed onto the front porch, and scrambled onto an old chair next to the window. The light inside houses was always so golden yellow. Oswald wondered if humans saved up sunshine and piped it through their lamps.

Joey had a book open on his lap, but stared ahead at the flickering television. Melvin slept next to him, his sides going in and out like a furry accordion.

Oswald gave their secret knock, *rat-a-tat-TAT*.

Joey smiled and started to open the window but was interrupted by his mother.

Just my luck. Why doesn't she go do something useful—like make lasagna? Oswald tried to squeeze through. Joey and his mom snapped their heads around at the noise.

"Joey . . . you are *not* going to let that critter in, are you?" His mother looked annoyed but was trying not to smile at the same time.

Oswald poked his snout through the cracked open window. "Good evening, Joey. It's good to be back. Might you get the newspaper for us? It's Wednesday, you know."

Joey nodded ever so slightly to Oswald, given his mother was so against this boy-possum friendship. Then he said to his mother, "Don't worry, I won't let him in." Like most people, Miss Ann didn't understand Animal.

"At least not while I'm looking, right? Now stop fooling around and finish your homework. Did you write that story? It's getting late."

"Yeah, it's done. I wrote a poem instead—it could be shorter."

"A poem? I didn't know you wrote poetry. May I read it?" His mother smiled for real this time.

"Um, I already put it in my backpack." That was the last thing Joey wanted—to have to endure his mother gushing over some dumb poem. "Anyway, it's Wednesday, Mom. Oswald needs to see Animal Watch." Joey said, unable to hold back his real intentions any longer. He dashed past his mother onto the porch.

"Honestly, Joey." Miss Ann stood in the doorway. Melvin wove out through her legs.

Mr. Edwards, an older man with a face like a kind and wise hound dog, sat reading on the front porch next door.

"Good evening, Mr. Edwards," Joey's mother said. "Do you still have today's paper? Joey wants to borrow it."

"Let me check." Mr. Edwards pushed up from his creaky chair and opened his front door. Sounds of a beginner keyboard player floated out.

"Lillian?" The keyboard sounds stopped. A few seconds later, Mrs. Edwards, a short woman with a halo of frizzy gray hair, and Zola, a huge, whiskery dog, came out.

"You done with today's paper?" Mr. Edwards said.

The dog ambled back into the house.

Joey laughed to himself, remembering Oswald asking if Mrs. Edwards's typically bright clothing was some sort of signaling system. Joey was glad she didn't get insulted when Oswald complimented her on her "nice round shape."

The big canine returned with the paper in her mouth.

"Thanks, Zola. Go on, take it to Joey," Mr. Edwards said.

Zola padded over to Miss Ann's house.

"All right now, Dr. Dolittle," Joey's mother said. "When you're done with your little meeting, I want you washed up and in bed in fifteen minutes. I have to leave a little before you tomorrow, early shift."

"Don't forget, we're here if you need anything, Joey," Mr. Edwards said.

"Thanks, Mr. Edwards," Joey said.

Miss Ann went inside.

Joey and the animals gathered round. Oswald, on the porch table, danced from paw to paw to paw to paw in what Joey called his happy dance.

"What does it say? Is it a headline?"

"Get off the paper, Oswald. I can't see," Joey said.

Oswald backed up and tried to hold still.

"Well?" Oswald cleared his throat. "How many possums break into the library?"

Joey skimmed the column: "Owl perched on a computer. . .ferret on a bus. . ."

Joey read on, but there was no mention of Oswald or his latest escapade.

Oswald's head and tail drooped. Melvin stretched, jumped off the chair, and gave his front paw a lick. "Better luck next time, Oz." He sauntered off the porch to the back of the house. Zola went home to the Edwardses' and Joey walked to the door.

"Good night, Oswald." The door closed behind Joey with an empty click. The night was quiet except for the sound of those infernal crickets.

When the last light went out in Joey's house, Oswald got a funny feeling in his stomach. He shivered, although it wasn't cold. He sighed and waddled off the porch and down the side of the house toward his home, an old wooden crate under the back deck. It was nice enough, with a red sweatshirt of Joey's folded into a bed, an upside-down plastic food container for a table, and a number of odds and ends, or "found objects" as Oswald called them, for decoration.

Suddenly, an idea swooshed into his marsupial brain like a small propeller plane buzzing a crowd. "Why didn't *I* think of that?"

He trotted up the steps onto the deck and squeezed through the cat flap. The big armchair inside looked like the perfect place for a nap, but first, he needed Melvin's help.

5

A BACKWARD MARCH TOWARD FAME

Melvin, who had already settled in for a snooze, yawned, his teeth glinting in the moonlight.

"I don't have a lot of time. Can you look up something for me on the Internet?"

Melvin stretched and leaped onto the desk in one graceful swoop. He turned on the computer. "What's the plan, Sam?"

"It's Oswald. Although some beings call me Oz, I do prefer Osw—"

"It's a saying, man." Melvin stared out the window for a moment. "What do you want me to look up?"

"I want to know if opossums are known for their poetry."

"Poetry? You *are* a piece of work." Melvin shook his head then tapped away on the keyboard.

"Fish carcass!" Melvin looked frustrated and typed some more. He must have been making mistakes. "Hairball!" Melvin said.

"No need to be coarse."

Melvin took a deep breath. Then he turned back to the keyboard and typed with one claw extended from each paw. The computer screen lit Melvin's large, handsome head. His whiskers glowed like fiber optics.

"You're in luck. Opossums are *not* famous for their poetry." Melvin gave an odd smile.

"Fabulous! I think Miss Ann likes poetry." Oswald clapped his front paws. "Might you be so kind as to get a pen and paper for me? Please?"

"Sure, man." Melvin pushed a few pieces of paper and a pen off the desk.

"Thank you, Melvin. You're a good friend."

Oswald started to write, but his pen kept poking holes through the paper into the carpet. After a few more tries, he

dragged the paper onto the dining table in the next room. Melvin carried the pen to him in his mouth without being asked.

Writing on the table worked much better. There was a moment of relative quiet; the only sounds were the pen scratching on paper and the summer's night orchestra of frogs and insects muffled through the windows. A train whistle sounded in the distance.

"Stop staring at me, I can't concentrate," Oswald told Melvin, who stood up, turned around twice, and re-curled himself in the opposite direction.

Oswald wrote some more.

"Please desist. You're sending bad vibrations—interfering with my brain waves."

Melvin sat up. "Not exactly a tsunami."

"What are you talking about?" Oswald said.

"Nothing. But I think I see a solution." Melvin trotted over to a blue plastic laundry basket on the floor.

"I bet the laundry basket would protect you from my stares and vibes."

Oswald clapped his front paws in agreement.

"And I know just the solution to protect those brain waves of yours."

The two worked together, tipping the basket and removing the few items, then hauling it from floor to chair, and chair to table. Then they flipped the basket over Oswald. This made a bright-blue plastic slatted hut over the struggling poet. Oswald started writing again, and Melvin jumped off the table and trotted off into the kitchen.

He returned with a fork in his mouth, jumped on the table and placed it on top of the upturned laundry basket.

Oswald stopped his writing, which was now going very well. "What on earth are you doing?"

Melvin explained that if there were metal objects on top of the upturned basket, they would absorb any "bio-electrical forces" that might be interfering with Oswald's brain waves and his brilliance. This sounded technical and complicated to Oswald, which convinced him it must be true. So Oswald returned to his writing while Melvin opened kitchen drawers and cupboards, carrying silverware and any metal objects he could manage.

Soon, there was a large pile of knives, forks and spoons, small pot lids, old keys, a rusty hinge, a broken watch, an empty cat-food can, and other odds and ends on top of the upside-down basket. Confident his brain waves were properly protected, Oswald wrote speedily, going backward with the pen in his back paw, covering page after page with scratchy marks. Meanwhile, Melvin slept in the armchair in the study, wearing another one of those odd smiles.

6

BUSTED

Joey was dreaming of a screeching, angry bird.

"Joseph Carlton Jones!" his mother yelled. "What on earth are you playing at?" He tumbled down the stairs in his pajamas and skidded to a stop next to his mother. There was the possum on the dining room table, under an upside-down laundry basket, topped with what looked like every kitchen utensil in the house. Underneath, Oswald crouched on a bed of papers, shifting from paw to paw.

"I've had enough of you and your critters, Joey." His mother seemed thoroughly vexed this time. "You know I have an early shift today—is that what this is about? My not cooking you breakfast?"

Joey shook his head and looked down. "No, Mom. I didn't do this. Honest."

"You didn't do this?" She studied her son's face. "You look like you believe it, too. So this creature did it? What—with Melvin's help?"

"Excuse me, but I find the word 'creature' offensive," Oswald said.

"Not now," Joey whispered out of the side of his mouth to Oswald.

Ann shook her head and looked at her watch. "I'm going to have to call Animal Control and get this possum relocated. I know it's been hard for you since Bradyn moved away. But you've got to make some friends—human ones. And this creature needs to be with other animals. Truly."

"Oh, Mom—please don't call Animal Control! It'll mess with his head. He doesn't like new places. He's shy," Joey begged. "I promise I won't ever, ever let him in again."

"Mm-hmm. I thought so." She stood with her arms crossed. "So you *did* let him in."

"No, ma'am, not this time . . . maybe before."

"Too late, I've heard enough. I'll see if Mr. or Mrs. Edwards can wait with you for Animal Control. I've got to go to work."

She dialed a number on her phone. Joey could hear the recorded announcement about which number to press and how "this message may be recorded."

"I should make a stew out of you." Miss Ann glared at Oswald, then marched outside.

Joey leaned in toward Oswald. "Now you've done it. You're going to be relocated."

Oswald clapped his forepaws. "Oh, this is splendid. She's calling Animal Control—that's marvelous!" His black eyes shone.

"Oh, man. This isn't good, Oswald. You're supposed to help me with my science project this weekend, remember?"

"Yes, yes. Don't be ridiculous. It's not due until the Wednesday after next. We have plenty of time, good fellow. And don't worry, this is Darnell's patch and he won't relocate me." Oswald paused, looked serious. "Now Joey, this is important. Make sure Darnell sees my poetry. This will surely get me into Animal Watch."

Joey lifted the laundry basket a few inches, careful not to dislodge all the metal things, and slid out the wad of papers. They were covered with jagged marks. "This mess?"

"That's no way to speak to your elders, Joey."

"But Oswald, you're only one year old."

◆ ◆ ◆

Mr. Edwards stood next to Joey in the dining room. Animal Control Officer Darnell Anderson clicked the cage shut and shoved a microchip scanner back in his pocket. Oswald peered out through the wire-mesh window.

"Yup, this guy's got quite a record. We only microchip them if we've been called for them at least three times, and this one . . . well, let's just say he's a frequent flyer." Darnell chuckled. He took out a digital logbook from another pocket and swiped through some pages. "The initial caller, Ms. Ann Jones—is that your mom?"

"Yes, sir."

"I see she requested relocation. We can do that."

Joey looked stricken despite Oswald's reassurance a few minutes ago.

"Wait, these papers. It looks like he was trying to write a message or something." Joey held them out to Darnell. Mr. Edwards and Darnell exchanged glances before Darnell took them.

"Thank you, young man. I'm sure our animal behavior team will be very interested."

Darnell took the cage outside, and Joey and Mr. Edwards followed. Darnell loaded the cage onto the front passenger seat of his van. Joey knew Oswald loved the tree-green van with the black-and-red writing on the sides. To Oswald, it was practically a limo.

Joey got an awful, hollow feeling in his stomach. Mr. Edwards stood next to him as they watched the van pull away.

"Don't worry. I bet he's back in time for dinner," Mr. Edwards said.

7

BARNARD HILL PARK

Darnell drove east on Perry Street, then turned left. Glimpses of houses, trees, and sky flicked by through the cage screen and van window. Darnell made more turns as he sped down the road. Oswald slid back and forth in the cage and started to feel sick.

"My goodness, Darnell. Is everything all right?"

Darnell didn't answer.

"Why so many turns, my good man?"

Darnell turned up the radio and revved up a hill.

Oswald shouted. "Excuse me, Darnell. Might you inform me of our route? I'm having trouble keeping track." Darnell still didn't answer.

The van slowed to a stop. Traffic swooshed by. In a few moments, they started off again down a longer road with a curve in it. Oswald could only see green and sky, then a few houses when Darnell stopped the van. He clicked open the cage top and light flooded in. Oswald stood on his hind paws and looked out the window.

"Where are we?"

Darnell reached behind his seat and retrieved a pink paper bag. "Lemon custard or Boston cream?"

"How lovely! Lemon custard, please!" Oswald did his happy dance. "You're going to love this, Darnell—*poetry*. This will most certainly get me into Animal Watch. I can hear my mother now—she always said I was destined for big things." Oswald gestured at the papers with his snout while he gripped the donut like a steering wheel.

Darnell glanced at the rumpled papers on the seat between them. "'Big things, eh? You mean besides your stomach? Look, every mother thinks her kid's a star. I know you lost her too young, but you've got to get a grip on something besides that donut." He chuckled, but Oswald didn't see what was so funny.

Oswald huffed. "I understand not everyone is naturally ambitious—I'm glad you're satisfied with your position, for example. But you have to admit, it's obvious I have considerably more talent than the average animal who gets their piffling antics reported in the newspaper. You know, this could help your career too," Oswald finished with a flourish.

Darnell shook his head as he swallowed the last of his donut. "You really are a piece of work, you little prehistoric nuisance—thinking you're so much better than everybody else." He arched an eyebrow. "But what can I expect—you don't even have a corpus callosum."

"That was uncalled for. You know I can't help my . . . brain . . . anatomy . . . " Oswald started acting woozy. "I . . . I don't feel well . . . " Oswald rolled his eyes back and slumped down in the cage.

"Don't go fainting on me." Darnell stroked Oswald's back. That felt nice. Oswald felt a little guilty faking a faint, but the problem was Darnell seemed to fall for it every time and was always nice about it. And it was much simpler than carrying on this discussion—after all, Oswald didn't want to make Darnell feel any worse. He hadn't meant to sound harsh, comparing their lives. Oswald promised himself to try to be kinder in the future.

"It's OK. You'll be all right," Darnell repeated over and over, giving him a perfect scratch behind the ears.

Oswald was enjoying the attention and forgot everything else for a moment. When he finally looked out the window, everything seemed unfamiliar. "Where are we? You never said."

"Barnard Hill Park."

Oswald chuckled. "Oh dear friend, you *are* confused. You've crossed the city line into Washington, DC, out of your jurisdiction."

"Exactly. Look, you should mix with more animals. Give this whole fame thing a rest. What do you think getting into Animal Watch would get you anyway? A big Hollywood deal?" Darnell flicked donut crumbs from his shirt.

Oswald's ears started to ring. "What? No. What about my poetry? An opossum writing poetry is a terrific story. Your name will get into the newspaper, too—as the one who 'found' me. You will report this, won't you?"

"Of course," Darnell said while looking at his watch. He snapped the cage lid shut so fast, Oswald had to duck to avoid bumping his head. Darnell swung the cage out of the van.

"Darnell, my good friend, I've learned my lesson. I give you my solemn promise."

The sound of Darnell's footfalls changed as he continued into the park. The smell of grass, earth, and trees wafted into the cage. Darnell put the cage down.

"Well done, Darnell. You've made an excellent point. Now let's go back to Mount Rainier."

Darnell opened the lid. Oswald looked up. His good human friend smiled. Oswald was about to tell him he missed some crumbs when he noticed the huge tree looming behind. Its thick branches reached up like strong, gnarled arms. The giant canopy of dark green leaves as big as a man's hands blotted out the sky. There was a large hollow halfway up. Oswald shuddered to think who might live there.

Darnell followed Oswald's gaze. "Great minds think alike. Eh, buddy? That hollow looks like a good place to start. You'll make a lot of friends here. The park's loaded with animals."

Oswald felt tired. His muscles felt heavy. He knew this meant he was going to faint for real this time. How embarrassing. Everything was getting blurry and sounded far away, but he could still make out a few things.

Darnell retrieved thin plastic gloves from his back pocket. He shook his head and lifted him out of the cage. "Pee-ew! Already? That fake death stink? Nice. At least you didn't do it in the van."

Darnell arranged Oswald in a pile of leaves at the base of the tree.

"You'll be fine. No one will mess with a smelly ole rotten possum. You'll come round soon enough. I will miss you, little buddy, but this is best for you." Darnell walked toward the van.

Oswald tried to say something, anything that would bring Darnell back, but by then he couldn't speak, move a muscle, or even blink an eye.

Oswald's world went dark.

8

IS THERE AN APP FOR THAT?

Oswald came to in the afternoon. With his eyes still closed, he lay on his back in the warm sunshine and drummed a little tune on his stomach. "Nothing beats the sun on the face and tum." He quite liked his little rhyme. Maybe he was a poet after all. He yawned, stretched, and opened his eyes, thinking of Miss Ann's lasagna. But his new reality doused him like a bucket of cold water. He was under that horrid tree in that awful park where Darnell left him. No, *abandoned* him. He thought nothing could be worse, until it was; something moved above him in the hole in the tree—something with eyes.

Oswald clamped his own eyes shut. He heard chattering and paws with claws scrambling down the rough bark. He stuck his tongue out, remembering to point it down, not up, hoping to look dead and uninteresting.

Multiple sets of paws padded toward him, most likely belonging to the tree dwellers. There were two, maybe three, voices. He wasn't sure why he wasn't scared enough to faint. Maybe it was because these critters were joking and laughing. He stayed still, not wanting to give himself away. Whoever they were, they were close now. He felt someone's hot breath when they sniffed him.

"Hey, Tiny. I didn't know you ordered takeout," one voice said. The two others snickered.

Oswald felt a warm nose on his flank.

"I don't know, Chuck. Looks like we'll have to cook him ourselves!" a second voice said, followed by laughter.

"Oh, Mo, cook him? On what? The cell phone?" the third voice said. "Is there an app for that?" The three rolled around, crunching the rain-starved grass and laughing.

Oswald couldn't take it. He blinked his eyes open to see who these fools were. Raccoons. Three of them. Oswald had always found raccoons a bit raucous and goofy for his taste, and these three were proving no different. Was one of them holding a cell phone? He must have imagined it. In any case, he clamped his eyes shut, hoping they'd lose interest and go away.

"Hey, he blinked. He's alive," Chuck said. Oswald felt noses and paws pushing and prodding him. He held tight, confident he could outwit these ridiculous creatures.

The three raccoons gave Oswald a full physical examination: they combed through his fur, moved his limbs this way and that, drew back his lips, and counted his teeth. This took real restraint on Oswald's part because they kept losing count, coming up with different numbers, and laughing. After a few tries, the three raccoons agreed he had fifty. One of them moved Oswald's jaw like he was a puppet, making him say silly things. That was it. Oswald sat bolt upright.

"Enough, gentlemen, enough! Show a New World marsupial a little respect." Oswald smoothed the fur on his face and down his middle.

The three raccoons jumped back. They all had the classic black mask markings on their faces, with tawny-brown coats and ringed tails of black and tan. One of them was quite massive, a good thirty-five pounds. The other two were a more ordinary size, and one of these had a chunk missing out of his ear.

"We were only trying to help," said Chuck, the one with the funny ear.

"I'm perfectly fine, and certainly don't need help from, well . . . your sort," Oswald said.

Chuck looked at Mo, who looked at Tiny, who shrugged his massive shoulders, his name being ironic.

Chuck spoke. "We've never seen you before. Need any help? I know what it's like to be stuck someplace new. Happened to me once, and if it hadn't been for the kindness of a stranger—"

"Oh, don't start with all that again." Mo shook his head at Chuck.

"Come on, you two," Tiny said. "I thought we were going to dinner, fried chicken—"

Mo interrupted, "I thought we agreed on garbage buffet."

"I feel like Chinese, we *never* have Chinese," Chuck whined.

Oswald followed the conversation like a three-way tennis match.

"Well, whatever we decide, you're welcome to join us," Tiny said over his friends' heads.

"No thank you, gentlemen. Let me introduce myself. I'm Oswald, the opossum of Perry Street. But most folks use the shorter term, 'possum,' although I find this a bit lackadaisical." He paused to see if the raccoons understood this big word, but they seemed to. "Oh, yes, sorry. I digress."

"Do you mean digest?" Mo said and poked Chuck.

"Digesting is much more fun than digressing," Chuck said and started to giggle again.

"Let the critter finish," Tiny said.

Oswald cleared his throat. "Yes, in any event, I have come here to, um, to contemplate the woodland. Yes, that's why I've come—for inspiration. I'm a writer, you see. A poet, soon to be published."

"I'm sure you are," Tiny said and gave his friends some sort of look.

"Well, we're not much on reading, have to admit," Chuck said.

Oswald brushed a twig from his shoulder. "Yes, I can see we travel in different circles."

"Come on, you guys," Tiny said. "Let's go get dinner, I'm hungry."

After Chuck and Mo stopped laughing, they ran to catch up with Tiny, who had lumbered across the grass toward the street. Tiny looked over his shoulder at Oswald one more time. "Should we bring you anything?"

"That's very kind, but I certainly won't be here when you get back. I'm afraid my services are needed in Mount Rainer." But the farther the raccoons ambled into the distance, the more Oswald felt lonely and even a little afraid. Without their boisterous company, he started to think about Joey. He wondered how he was, and what he might be doing. He wondered if Joey was watching a good movie without him. But he knew the boy wouldn't be so thoughtless.

Joey made as much noise as possible putting the dishes in the dishwasher.

"Easy, Joey. You'll break something," Ann said as she tucked leftovers into the fridge.

"Who cares?" Joey dropped a metal lid into the sink with a satisfying clatter. Ann whirled around and glared at him.

"Just stop it, Joey! You need to get a grip. I'm *not* sorry I had that possum removed. You can't have them crawling all over the house, honey. You *know* that."

Joey didn't say anything, but put a pot in the sink gently.

After a patch of quiet with Ann exhaling loudly, and Joey working hard to *not* say what he was thinking, Ann broke the silence. She leaned against the counter, holding a washed pot and a dish towel.

"Well, I have to say, this is exactly why I never liked you having just one good friend. I'm sorry Bradyn moved away. I know this has been really hard on you. But things change in life, Joey. It's something we all have to learn to deal with." She tried to put her hand on his shoulder, but he dodged her touch. "Come on. When you're older, you can go visit him in Chicago, I promise. But now you need to make more human—"

"Mr. Edwards said Oswald would be back before dinner, and he's not! Something must be wrong. Now you've really done it!"

Ann started to say something, but Joey interrupted. He couldn't hold back any longer. "You send *everyone* way. *Don't* you? First Dad, and now Oswald!"

"Oh, Joey," was all she said as Joey stormed out of the kitchen.

9

A CHANGE OF HEART

Early the next morning, on Friday, Oswald sat under the tree, which no longer looked as scary. He watched Tiny, Mo, and Chuck saunter, waddle, and stroll across the grass in his direction. The morning dew was welcome in this unusually hot, dry spring.

The three raccoons looked woozy, as though they might be drunk. But, as they got nearer it became clear their hangovers were from food, not drink. Their bellies looked like they might burst. Oswald overheard them talking about the night. They had eaten a number of times: the Shepherd Street garbage buffet—"all you can eat," Chuck reminded them, the fried chicken place, and the Chinese takeout.

"Oh yes, and don't forget—Twenty-Second Street Pizza," Tiny said and patted his belly like it was a friend. Chuck and Mo nodded their agreement.

If their inane conversation wasn't enough, their copious burps and farts irked Oswald to no end. Oswald hated to even think the word, but these fellows were . . . ordinary.

Chuck, the one with the lopped-off ear, saw Oswald first. "Hi! So you've decided to stay. We were hoping you were, weren't we?" He swiped his paw at his friends. Tiny looked neutral, and Mo looked annoyed.

"Chuck, just because that dog helped you that *one* time when you were stuck in that fence doesn't mean we have to help every idiot," Mo said.

"I beg your pardon!" Oswald said.

"Come on, Mo. You know Animal Control dumped him here—it's not his fault. And that dog probably *did* save Chuck's furry butt. Taught us all a lesson about the kindness of strangers, eh?" Tiny said.

Mo huffed, "Well, it's fine if he stays. It's a free country. But he can't fit in our den."

Chuck looked at Oswald as though he was sorry he had to hear all that.

"Now my good fellows, there is no need to worry. I've merely stayed to do a bit more research. I fully understand the issue of limited resources and will return to my own nest shortly. In fact, I have some important meetings this weekend with a Mr. Joseph—"

Mo raised an eyebrow. "Lost, are we?"

Oswald spluttered.

Tiny put his paw around Oswald's shoulder. Oswald tried not to show how uncomfortable this made him.

"Don't be embarrassed. You were pretty much kidnapped. We can help," Tiny said.

Oswald wriggled out from under Tiny's limb. "So kind, but no need, I assure you. I am well versed with my local geography and"—Oswald tapped his head—"I have MPS, a marsupial positioning system."

Tiny shrugged his broad furry shoulders and yawned. "It's your life."

"We can't just leave him on his own," Chuck said.

"Why not?" Mo said and prodded Chuck toward the tree. The two started their ascent while arguing about whether or not they should help Oswald.

"See you later, Oswald. You know where we are if you need anything," Tiny said then lumbered up the tree behind his friends.

Oswald was keen to get back to Joey's house so they could work on his school project, "The Tale of Tails." They were making a big poster with drawings and information about all sorts of tails and how they worked. Oswald would go to school that day with Joey and demonstrate his own prehensile tail. This would be sure to get Joey extra credit.

For the rest of Friday, Oswald fought his natural desire to sleep during the day and walked in a straight line from the tree. He marked his path with small twigs he found along the way, even though he wouldn't be coming back. *Just good policy.* Eventually, he found himself on a street lined with tidy brick houses. He wasn't sure which way to go. Then he smelled some luscious garbage. *Need to fuel the brain for optimal thinking.* After enjoying some sandwich crusts and licking out a yogurt container, he realized it was getting dark and he was getting sleepy. *Maybe Miss Ann is right—it might be good for Joey to be a bit more independent from me. I'll go home tomorrow.* Oswald waddled back to the tree, following the twigs that were mostly still there. *That's odd. They're not in a straight line at all.* He found a hollow under some nearby shrubs to sleep in.

"I don't see him." Chuck's disappointed voice woke Oswald early Saturday morning. Oswald peeked through the branches and saw the three raccoons walking toward their tree. *After another night of gluttony, no doubt.*

Tiny clapped Chuck on the back. "Cheer up, buddy. That's good news for Oswald."

Oswald waited for them to climb the tree and into their hollow before venturing out.

The next three days, through Monday, went much the same for Oswald. He would walk out from the big tree in what he thought was a straight line, marking his path with twigs, only to find the twigs in curves and swirls when he retraced his steps. Plus, all the streets and houses started to look the same, and none of them were Perry Street, where Joey lived. At least he was getting to know where all the best garbage cans were.

By Monday morning, Oswald decided it takes a well-adjusted animal to know when to ask for help. He came out of the shrub as the raccoons walked across the grass toward their home.

"Good morning, kind sirs—" Oswald started.

Chuck rushed up and hugged him. "You're here! You've decided to stay!"

"Oh brother," Mo said and rolled his eyes.

"Are you OK?" Tiny said.

"Well, as a matter of fact I could use your help. I was wondering if you might call Joey, I mean Mr. Joseph Jones, on your cell phone?"

"Sure, no problem," Tiny said and retrieved the phone from their den.

"Can I do it, please? Please? I LOVE pushing buttons," Chuck said.

"You certainly do," Mo said.

Tiny held the phone above their heads. "I'll do it—what's the number?"

Oswald coughed and spluttered. "I am ever so sorry for the unnecessary inconvenience. I just realized that I don't need to make the call after all."

"Uh-huh. Don't know the number, do you?" Mo gave a long whistle. "You are a piece of work, man. You really are."

Oswald was stunned into an uncharacteristic silence. This was not the first time he'd heard this about himself. He wasn't sure exactly what they meant, but the words felt like a bruise without a punch, like a sting without a bee. He made his excuses and wandered off.

"Hey, Oswald. Don't take Mo seriously." Chuck trotted after him.

But, saying he had a headache, Oswald excused himself and waddled off into the thick undergrowth of the grassy park.

By Tuesday morning, Oswald started to panic. Joey's project was due in a little over a week. Not only that, but he was sure the other animals at Miss Ann's house would be a bit lost without him by now. Plus, Oswald needed to find someone with a newspaper to read the Animal Watch column tomorrow. His poetry would no doubt be in it.

He swallowed his pride and approached the raccoons.

"Well, well, well. Look what the cat dragged in," Mo said. They were walking back from their night's food sojourn.

"Good morning, good fellows. I can assure you, no feline, domestic or otherwise, dragged me anywhere."

After a number of discussions about where Perry Street might be, which all ended with the raccoons either rolling about in the grass laughing, or climbing into a nearby garbage can for a snack, Tiny thought to use their cell phone. It took a few tries, during which they kept bumping heads, as the three raccoons all tried to see the map on the phone at the same time. It turned out Perry Street was close. But to get there, you had to cross busy Eastern Avenue.

"OK everybody, ready to go find Perry Street? The dumpsters in that neighborhood are famous—wouldn't mind checking them out afterward," Tiny said. Chuck and Mo nodded their agreement, and they all fell in line behind Tiny. They padded down Twenty-Fourth Street then onto Randolph. It was evening, the time a lot of humans came back from work, as far as Oswald understood. A few people nodded hello, but none spoke Animal. Most ignored them. After about ten more minutes, they reached Eastern Avenue. The cars whizzed by. It might as well have been the Nile River filled with crocodiles—Oswald started to feel faint.

Three times, Tiny tried to get the others to follow him when the coast was clear, but by the time they all reached the curb, a car or truck barreled through, blowing their fur back.

"Gentlemen, I must warn you, I think I'm about to faint, it is ever so . . . embarrass . . . ing."

Chuck rushed over and caught him by the shoulders.

"Oh, there you go again, getting too involved," Mo said. Mo argued with Chuck, who laid Oswald down under a bush.

Then Tiny pointed to something hanging above the street and exclaimed, "That's it. That's the answer!"

They all looked where Tiny had been staring. People walked to the edge of the sidewalk and stopped, looking upward. Then at the same time, without any of the humans saying anything or giving any sort of obvious signal, they all crossed Eastern Avenue. Every car, bus, truck, and van stopped and waited in line while the humans crossed.

"I get it," Tiny said. "Look, that thing controls the cars!"

"What thing? Oh, that thing? I thought it was a Christmas decoration they forgot to take down," Chuck said.

Tiny sat on the edge of the grass by the sidewalk and studied the "thing" and the people, as though he were a *National Geographic* wildlife photographer. The others huddled at his sides.

Another human walked up and joined others standing on the sidewalk. They all stared at the thing. The brightest light changed position, from the top to the bottom—*Green,* one of the few colors raccoons can see. The people walked across the street.

Tiny charged ahead. "Come on, this is our chance!" Chuck, Mo, and Oswald fell in line. One woman gave a little shriek; another said, "How cute."

On the other side of the road, the raccoons all high-fived one another then, seeing Oswald's distaste, they each shook his paw. They discussed this amazing technology that stopped cars, but cut it short when Oswald looked up. "*That's* where I live!"

With Miss Ann and Joey's house in sight, Oswald broke into a run. Tiny, Mo, and Chuck loped after him, hooraying and whooping. Oswald stopped in front of the house, causing a raccoon pile-up on top of him and setting the threesome off, laughing once again. Oswald untangled himself from the animal heap and extended a paw to Tiny.

"Thank you, thank you, all." He gave a little bow. "You've been ever so kind, in spite of my . . . " He cleared his throat. "My, um, not always being as gracious, as . . . well . . . I might have been."

The porch was vacant except for an empty glass. Yellow light came from the living room window. Mr. Edwards was on his porch next door in his old wicker chair.

"I'd offer you some refreshments, but I don't have much on paw," Oswald said, hoping they wouldn't stay. He had lots to catch up on and was, well, exhausted.

"Do you have any grapes? I love grapes!" Chuck asked, doing a little jig.

Tiny grabbed Chuck by the elbow and led him away. "Why don't we stop by another time?" Tiny said. "You've got our number, right? Give us a holler. We'll do something sometime."

"Yes, I will call you, gentlemen. I would be delighted to see you again." Oswald thought he might even mean it.

The raccoons turned back toward Eastern Avenue, discussing where these famous dumpsters might be, and Oswald started up the stairs. He needed to tell Melvin everything that had happened and find out what he'd missed. But Melvin was nowhere in sight, and the house was now completely dark. Then it dawned on Oswald—maybe they'd all forgotten about him by now. Maybe they had got on with their lives without him.

10

THE VOICE OF THE STORM

"Oswald, Oswald, OSWALD . . . "

Oswald dreamt he'd won a great poetry prize and everyone was chanting his name. He walked on stage and took a deep bow. When he opened his mouth to give his thank-you speech, he was drowned out by people shouting his name.

"Oswald. OSWALD . . . "

He was flattered, but after a while he thought, *How rude*, and tried to quiet the crowd. But the words wouldn't come out of his mouth.

"OSWALD."

Wait. Someone *was* calling his name, over and over again.

"My goodness, do I have to do *everything* around here?"

He groaned out of bed, combed his face, and checked his teeth in his reflection in the shiny can lid Joey had nailed on the wall for him. He posed at different angles, considering the best photo for his first book of poetry. But the chanting continued. He squeezed out of the front door of his crate and climbed out from under the deck.

Oswald blinked in the morning sun. On top of the fence between Joey's and the Edwardses' backyards floated the head of a large, whiskery dog. From the dog's mouth came: "OS-WALD, Oswald."

Oswald trotted to the edge of the deck nearest to the fence. "Good morning, dear Zola. It's good to see you, too. But please, you mustn't make such a fuss."

The back door to the house opened. Melvin slithered out, followed by Miss Ann, then Joey.

"Hush, Zola. Stop all that barking," Miss Ann said.

Zola stopped, cocked her head to one side, and sat down, her head still visible above the low fence.

"Yo, Oswald. You're back!" Joey punched the air, stopping when he saw his mother's face.

Melvin settled on the warm wood of the deck, between Joey and Oswald. "Hey, Oz. How you doing?"

"I'm fine, thank you very much. I've been away doing research for my poetry—"

Melvin arched an eyebrow, looked right at Oswald. "Right. Animal Control took you to a regular old poetry party. I bet. Win any prizes?"

Miss Ann looked at Joey. "How can you be sure this is the same possum? They promised they'd relocate it."

Oswald cleared his throat. "*Him,* not 'it'."

Joey's grin was almost as wide as an opossum's. "I *know* it's him." Joey continued, "You can identify individual possums, well, the kind we have here, *Didelphis virginiana,* by the patterns of black and white on their ears. And they're immune to snake venom, and they can't get rabies, and their babies develop in their pouches like kangaroos, and—"

"All right already, Joey," his mom said.

"And they can wrap their tails around tree branches, but once they're grown, they can't really hang by their tails, and then there's their really cool opposable big toe, like our thumbs but on their back paws—"

"JOEY!"

"Right, sorry."

"I'm off, guys. Got to go to work as usual. If that's all right with everyone?" Miss Ann looked at each animal in turn, then Joey, then shook her head. "What am I doing? I'm getting as bad as you, talking to the animals." She lifted Joey's wrist and tapped his watch. "Twenty minutes, mister, and you're off to school."

"Yes, ma'am. Can I eat my breakfast out here?"

"I guess so, but no feeding that creature. Understand? And don't forget to lock the doors behind you."

Joey shared his breakfast with Zola, Melvin, and Oswald, while Oswald told them all about his adventures on the other side of Eastern Avenue. Joey's face changed expression as Oswald told him about the scary parts (being dropped in the "untamed forest"), the funny parts (the three raccoons), and the interesting parts, like the raccoons having a cell phone. Oswald started to tell them about the fascinating signaling device hanging over the intersection, when Joey looked at his watch and jumped up.

"Tell me all about it after school. I gotta go." Joey ran back into the house, leaving the dirty breakfast dishes behind and tipping over Melvin's bowl. The clatter roused Zola, who had moved to her spot in the Edwardses' backyard and dozed off. "Nice to have you back, Oswald. See you all later." She meandered into the Edwardses' house.

"Let's bring this stuff in, so Joey doesn't get into trouble," Melvin said.

Oswald pushed the breakfast dishes through the cat flap while Melvin held it open with his back.

They couldn't open the dishwasher and decided against turning on the faucet to wash the dishes, in case they forgot to turn it off. So they licked the dishes clean and put them away. Oswald had forgotten how nice it was to work with Melvin.

Afterward, the two settled in the study. Oswald chose a sunny patch on the carpet for a nap. Melvin took the armchair. The rest of the day poured over Oswald like maple syrup over warm pancakes. All the regular things seemed extra nice. Joey came home from school. Melvin kept Joey company while he did his homework; Oswald relaxed in the yard. Joey and his mom had dinner, and Joey snuck some lasagna to Oswald.

After dinner, Zola joined Oswald and Melvin to watch the world go by from the front porch.

"Everything seems lovelier than I remember," Oswald said.

"Yes, the bad times make the good ones shine. Don't you think, Zola?" Melvin said.

The sky darkened with thick gray clouds, and a wind whipped up.

Zola looked as though she were watching a movie that no one else could see. Different expressions washed over her scarred face. Zola wouldn't talk about her past—Oswald thought this was stubborn of her.

"Yes indeed," Zola said.

Evening birds darted through the air, squirrels climbed trees; it seemed everyone was readying for the storm. The crickets were silent.

"Anyway, as I was saying, my adventure could not have been more fruitful."

"Yes, possums like fruit. I've never enjoyed it much myself," Zola said.

"What? No, it's an expression," Oswald gently corrected.

"Here we go," Melvin groused.

"Oh, I almost forgot. Isn't it Wednesday today?" Oswald said.

"It is. I'll get the paper." Zola trotted back to her house and nosed the screen door open. Melvin sat in the front yard, doing what looked a lot like nothing.

"Melvin, might you be so kind as to go get Joey?" Oswald said. "You know I have trouble reading the small print in newspapers."

Melvin sloped off toward the back of the house.

A few minutes later, the four reconvened on the porch.

Joey shivered and looked at the sky. "We better hurry." Charcoal clouds blocked any sign of the moon or stars.

They settled into their usual places on or around the table. Joey got up and switched on the porch light. The wind jabbed them with chilly blasts. The newspaper flapped.

"Can't you find it? Maybe it's a headline," Oswald said.

Joey leaned on the pages to keep them from blowing around.

"Well?" Oswald yelled to be heard.

"I'm looking as fast as I can. Here it is."

As Joey was about to read Animal Watch, the page jerked up on a gust of wind.

"No! Joey, get it," Oswald said.

"What am I supposed to do—fly up and grab it?" Joey hollered. The four friends looked up, helpless. The paper danced on the wind, up, up, up—then disappeared into the darkness.

Seconds later, there was a sound of tearing newspaper, and a thump on the roof. Then a sound, like a sad saxophone. You could smell the coming rain. Melvin's fur stood on end. Oswald felt a faint coming on, and crumpled onto the tabletop, unable to move his limbs. Joey lifted his possum friend and tucked him into a basket in a far corner of the porch. He could still hear and see, but he couldn't make a sound. Melvin meowed by the door, his eyes as big as pies. Joey creaked it open, and Melvin slithered in. Zola stood at attention, hackles up.

The skies opened.

Over the storm, the sounds started again, like hopelessness without words. Melvin pressed against the living room window, looking out.

Zola nodded toward her house. "I'll go get Mr. Edwards. He'll bring his ladder."

The rain blew in. The temperature dropped. More eerie sounds came from above.

The screen door opened. Miss Ann stood silhouetted in a slice of light, her red curls a halo above her straight shoulders. "What in the Lord's name is going on out here?"

Joey shrugged.

Mr. Edwards appeared out of the darkness holding a ladder, Zola by his side.

"Evening, Miss Ann." He leaned the ladder against the porch roof and tested it. Zola sat down, her face slick with rain.

"Honestly, Mr. Edwards, let me climb up there. Did Joey put you up to this?"

"No, I'm all right. Something's landed up there—sounds like it's hurt."

"At least let me spot you."

The odd sounds continued.

They all watched as Mr. Edwards disappeared up the ladder.

"You all right up there?" Miss Ann said, but he didn't respond.

Mr. Edwards made his way down, cradling something about the size of two footballs, a mix of white, gray, black, and pink.

He stepped onto the porch, and Joey pulled out a chair for him.

This was the last thing Oswald remembered before the faint took him over completely. *Looks like an extra-large*

football with feathers on it. Probably some ill-advised child's idea of a joke, was the last thing he had a chance to think, and then he was out.

◆ ◆ ◆

"Is it alive?" Joey said.

Mr. Edwards nodded.

"I'll be right back," Miss Ann said.

After a moment that was quiet except for the voice of the storm, Miss Ann returned with the blue plastic laundry basket and towels. She settled herself in the other chair with the basket on her lap. Mr. Edwards arranged the large bird in it. It held its head under its wing and trembled. Miss Ann stroked its feathered back.

"Everything's going to be all right. Don't you worry, now."

After a few minutes, she started to sing an old lullaby. One by one, the others began singing along. Zola added the gentlest of howls. The bird stopped trembling, took its head out from under its wing, and joined in with the same sad sounds as before. There were tears in everyone's eyes. Everyone except for Oswald, who remained in a faint in the basket.

11

A BIGGER STORY

The next morning, Oswald awoke to the sound of people on Miss Ann's porch. There was a man with a camera and a woman. They both had ID cards around their necks. The woman rang the doorbell.

"Will this be an Animal Watch story?" the man asked.

"I don't know. It could be bigger. We'll see," the woman said.

Miss Ann opened the door.

Oswald almost levitated with excitement. *I knew it, I knew it.* He had trouble getting out of the basket and rocked back and forth, spilling out on his third try. He scrambled up to the front door, just as it latched shut. He leaned his ear against the door to listen.

"Of course. Why don't we go on the back deck, so you can take some pictures," Miss Ann said.

Isn't that lovely. They're going to take photographs. They must think I'm in bed under the deck—anyone could make that mistake.

He stumbled down the porch steps, stopped to study his reflection in a puddle, fixed his fur, then scurried toward the back of the house.

When he got to the deck, he couldn't believe what he heard.

"Yes, this is the goose that crashed onto our porch roof last night, during the storm," Miss Ann said. Oswald heard the clicking of the camera.

"Let's get a shot of the person who saved the goose, holding the bird," the woman reporter said.

"That's Mr. Edwards," Miss Ann said.

"No, it was a group effort," Mr. Edwards said.

Oswald walked up a couple of steps and peered onto the deck.

When did Mr. Edwards come over? I must have slept through that, too. Oswald didn't like being out of the loop. The goose was an odd-looking thing. It had pink webbed feet and a black neck that looked too long for the rest of it.

The woman reporter arranged them all for the photo, Joey happily crowding in.

"Ms. Jones, how about you sit with the goose on your lap, and Mr. Edwards, you stand behind," the photographer said, but Joey interrupted him.

"It's Naja. Her name is Naja."

"OK, Naja it is," the photographer said as he clicked away.

Off to the side, Oswald didn't see what all the fuss was about. Why on earth would the newspaper want her picture? What had the goose done to deserve all this fuss? After all he'd been through, now a total stranger, out of nowhere, was getting her picture in the paper?

Joey noticed Oswald peering over the deck. He jumped up. "Let's have Oswald in the picture, too. He was there."

Everyone looked at Oswald. "I guess I could fit in a quick photo shoot this morning." But it seemed the two reporters, like Miss Ann, couldn't understand Animal, because they acted as though he hadn't said anything.

The reporter looked nervous. "That big old rat? I don't know . . . "

"A *rat*? Who does she think he is? What a toadstool!"

"Oswald, that's not very nice," Joey said.

"Your son speaks Animal?" asked the photographer.

"Not that there's anything wrong with being a rat, of course," Oswald said to Joey.

"Not now," Joey said out of the side of his mouth to Oswald.

Miss Ann gave an odd laugh and walked over to Joey. She put an arm around him, blocking Oswald's view. "He's our regular Dr. Dolittle all right. Understands Animal better than most people." She gave Joey a little squeeze. "Come on, boo." Miss Ann guided Joey toward Mr. Edwards, the photographer, and that weird big bird in the blue plastic laundry basket.

"Not *my* blue plastic basket." Oswald bustled up the final step, waddled over to the basket, and sank his teeth into the plastic. "Come on—fly away, you interfering, egg-laying vertebrate!" He braced all four paws and tugged. His strength surprised him. He tugged again, and the basketful of bird teetered on the edge of the deck. The bird squawked and flapped one wing. Mr. Edwards and Joey grabbed the basket from the other side and ripped it away from Oswald.

"Don't! Her wing is broken, Oswald. That'll really hurt!" Joey yelped.

Oswald blinked. "How was I to know?" He hadn't meant to hurt her, only inspire her to leave.

Mr. Edwards returned the basket of goose to Miss Ann.

"Don't worry, I'll take care of him. He's a real nuisance, that possum," Mr. Edwards said. He chased Oswald down the steps and under the deck. Oswald turned around to give Mr. Edwards a piece of his mind but stopped before he got a word out. Mr. Edwards's face looked large as he crouched down and glared. He whispered, but it sounded more like a deep growl.

"The newspaper you all lost hold of nearly killed that poor bird."

"Ah well, maybe her number was up? Her goose would have been cooked, as they say," Oswald snickered.

Mr. Edwards shook his head. "OK, Oswald, I'm going to say this once. You keep this up and it's over. The end. Next stop, the big porch in the sky."

And with that, Mr. Edwards disappeared.

Oswald paced under the deck. *Probably best to stay out of sight for a while. Let them come to their senses.* He could hear what was happening on top of the deck and could see glimpses between the boards.

The photographer took a bunch of pictures. Then the lady reporter talked to Miss Ann and Mr. Edwards, asking them what they knew about such "cross-breed geese." He heard the words "Canada" and "pink-footed."

Finally, the humans left. Zola stayed behind with Melvin and that stupid bird. Oswald clambered up onto the deck. *Surely Melvin and Zola will also be horrified at all this nonsense over a bird.*

But Oswald's day was about to get worse. There they were—Melvin and Zola—gathered around this goose, listening to her tell a story as though it were the most amazing adventure they'd ever heard.

12

A CANDID CANINE

Oswald joined his friends on the deck, leaned against the railing, and draped his front limbs on top of his belly. "Melvin, Zola, please, what's going on? Has this bird put a spell on you?"

"Shh." Melvin waved his friend away. "She was just getting to the good parts. I want to hear this."

"Melvin, have you been in the catnip again? Come on, dear boy. This is a *bird*. Remember roast chicken? I hear goose is lovely with a—"

"Honk!" was the first thing the goose said to Oswald.

"Oswald, stop it. Don't upset her—she's been through enough," Zola said.

Oswald couldn't believe his ears. "Zola, not you, too?"

Zola got up and in two large steps stood over Oswald like a tent made out of dog. Oswald shuddered. Zola bent down and gently picked him up by the scruff of his neck.

"Put me down this minute. I will not stand for this," Oswald protested while paddling his four limbs in the air.

Zola carried Oswald to the back of the yard, reached her head over the fence as far as she could, and dropped the possum about three feet from the ground.

Oswald landed on soft weeds.

Zola lowered herself on the other side of the fence, bringing her head level with Oswald's.

"Oh, dear Zola, I do hope you realize I was merely joking. Of course I'm interested in what that bird—"

"Stop," Zola barked. Oswald jumped back. He looked past Zola at the deck. Melvin sat on the railing, watching them, his tail swished back and forth.

"Hurry up, Zola. I want to hear the rest." Melvin jumped down and disappeared from view.

Zola looked right into Oswald's eyes. "Oswald, you know I like you."

Oswald nodded. "I cherish our friendship too, dear Zola."

"But you crossed a line this time. You could have really hurt that poor goose, and she's already injured. Maybe now's a good time for a vacation."

"But I've been away—seen the world, my candid canine friend."

Zola shook her scruffy head, got up stiffly, and walked back to the deck.

Oswald scurried back and forth along the fence. "You misunderstood me. I was merely trying to remedy a mix-up—save all of you embarrassment. Surely, the newspaper people came for *me*." Oswald said this and a whole lot more until he finally realized a frightening fact: *no one is listening to me.*

13

BIT OF A PREDICAMENT

Oswald knew his friends weren't serious. As soon as he made it big, he would buy a huge house where they'd all have their own rooms—Joey, Miss Ann, Melvin, and himself, plus a few guest rooms. Zola could stay over anytime she wanted. They'd have a Jacuzzi and maybe a mud bath although he wasn't sure what that was, and a full-time cook. Definitely a full-time cook.

He went over to the Edwardses' back fence and rooted around for the gap he used to use when he was younger. He squeezed through—it had been a long time.

How lovely. He'd forgotten how magical the Edwardses' garden was, an oasis of green paths, flowering bushes, and jasmine-covered archways.

He waddled down the garden path, turned left, and pressed through azalea bushes to the fence between the Edwardses' and the Joneses' yards. His friends' voices drifted over.

"He's OK, really, but he does get on my nerves sometimes," Zola said.

"*Your* nerves?" Melvin said. "Man, oh, man. He is one high-maintenance marsupial."

There was a pause. Oswald felt bad. *Is that a bumper sticker or something? Am I truly that difficult?*

"Then why are you friends with him?" Naja the goose asked.

Oswald dove through the old fence hole where he first entered Miss Ann's garden when he was a little joey himself, not long out of his mother's pouch. It had been lonely being the only baby to survive from that litter, and his mother was glad he'd found Joey and Melvin as friends. That was all a few months before Oswald's mother died in an unfortunate accident with a delivery truck.

But now that Oswald was fully grown, the fence panel was too snug. He was stuck halfway through the fence. At least he was hidden under a daisy bush. He could see them pretty well if he tilted his head and looked through the stems.

"What was that?" Zola woofed.

Melvin rolled on his back and licked a spot on his side. Naja, still sitting in Oswald's blue basket, craned her neck and looked around. Oswald held still; he didn't make a sound.

"Someone from a rescue center's coming soon for you, Naja. I heard Miss Ann on the phone," Melvin said.

"Yes, Naja, please go on—finish what you were telling us," Zola said.

Oh bother, I'm going to have to hear all this rubbish.

"You see, I'm a cross-breed goose. My father was a pink-footed and my mother was a Canada goose. He'd made a wrong turn one year on his migration from Greenland to Great Britain and ended up in New Jersey instead."

"That's some wrong turn," Melvin said.

"I know. He was a stubborn old bird. It was only after another eight hundred miles that he admitted he was lost."

Zola gave a soft whistle. "Poor guy. He must have been exhausted."

"He was. He wound up in a place called Schlegel Lake." Naja stretched and tried to flap her wings but winced and stopped. "There were a number of Canada geese there, and my dad fell in love with my mother, but her flock never accepted him."

Yes, yes . . . we all feel misunderstood at some point. I know what it's like to grow up the only one of your kind. But come on, move on. I have, Oswald thought.

"You see, everyone in a flock usually looks and acts the same. Not only did my father look and act different, he sounded different, too." Naja trailed off, made a sound between a wheeze and a honk, and put her head under her wing.

"What is it?" Zola said and pawed at the blue slatted basket.

"I've never fit in. My feet and beak are too pink for the Canada geese. My honk doesn't sound right. My neck's too long for the rest of me. All the other goslings picked on me." She shuddered.

"Why not join a pink-footed flock?" asked Zola.

"There's no guarantee they'd accept me either. And anyway, I can't fly all the way to Greenland on my own."

They were all quiet for a moment.

For goodness' sake, take a bus, Oswald thought.

Naja sat up in the basket. "But it hasn't been all bad. If I hadn't crashed, I wouldn't have met you two, and Miss Ann and Joey. You've all been so kind. I'm sorry I have to leave."

"Why don't you come back once your wing is healed?" Zola said.

Oswald thought he might faint, or at least throw up. He felt more than left out, he felt like he never existed.

"But Naja, I don't understand. Why were you flying this far from New Jersey to begin with?" Melvin asked.

"I heard there were some groups of mixed-breed birds in Virginia. I was heading down there when the storm hit," Naja said.

Well, I've heard plenty. Besides, I'm hungry. I wonder if Mrs. Edwards might have a snack. She used to feed me . . . after the accident.

But when he tried to back out of the fence hole, he couldn't—he was stuck. He tried pushing through and backing out—nothing. *How humiliating.* He had no choice, but as he was about to holler for help, he heard Miss Ann's voice from the deck.

"Yes, here she is. My son Joey speaks Animal. She said her name is Naja, obviously a girl."

"Well then, Naja, nice to meet you." Oswald didn't recognize this other woman's voice. "You and your son are welcome to come and visit her and us at the center." He parted the daisies to look, no longer worried about being seen.

"Thank you. I think Joey would like that," she said.

Miss Ann is willing to drive all the way to who knows where to see a goose she just met? The animal worker lifted the goose from the basket into a transport cage. With the goose out of the way, Oswald figured it was safe to rejoin his friends and called out. He made a hissing noise, like bacon sizzling but louder.

The woman looked out into the yard. "Sounds like a possum. Wonder if it's in distress?"

This is hopeful. Oswald made more sizzling-hissing sounds.

Miss Ann sighed. "In that case, I bet I know who it is. We have a troublesome one around here. We're working on relocating him."

"I'm afraid I only work with fowl," the woman said. "But I can call my colleague."

"Don't worry. We'll handle it. Thanks for helping with Naja. She is awfully sweet."

The woman clicked the transport cage shut, music to Oswald's ears. He waited through the good-byes and until he heard the van drive away.

"Excuse me, Miss Ann, Zola, Melvin? Can any of you hear me? If you would be so kind, I'm afraid I'm in a bit of a predicament."

The stems of the daisies parted. Miss Ann looked down at him, one hand on her hip.

"You're not welcome here anymore." She whipped a dish towel from her back pocket, covered his face, and pushed him backward through the fence hole.

"Miss Ann, *please,* you are pushing in the wrong direction." Oswald didn't like having his face covered. "Certainly there's a better way," came out in muffled tones.

"Please don't bite me," Miss Ann said, which cut through Oswald like a laser. He would never bite anyone, not unless his life depended on it. And he would *never* bite Joey or Miss Ann.

All of a sudden, he popped back through the fence into the Edwardses' yard. Oswald brushed himself off and looked at Miss Ann through the hole. He knew she couldn't understand Animal, but he couldn't stop from explaining himself.

"I am astounded that you would think I would ever bite you. Why don't we sit down sometime, get to know each other better? Possibly, say, over a dinner?"

Miss Ann remained crouched down, looking at him through the hole. "I know you're trying to tell me something."

She stood up. All Oswald could see now were her sneakers. "We could have takeout. I didn't mean to presume you would cook."

And then, all at once, a bright-orange-and-purple plastic tray came down across the hole.

14

RIGHT AND OUT OF SIGHT

Jazz piano music drifted from the Edwardses' bungalow. *Ah, Lillian's home.* Oswald went to their back screen door and banged his forehead against the lower panel. The music stopped. A beat later, Lillian appeared on the other side. She looked out into the backyard. When Oswald knocked again, she looked down and laughed. "Oh, it's you."

Oswald wasn't sure how to take Lillian sometimes. He gave a little bow. "Yes, sorry to bother you. I wonder if you might have a snack you could spare?" Lillian understood Animal.

"You know I don't believe in feeding wild animals, not once you're grown. It's not good for you."

"I can assure you I'm not wild." He sniffed the air. "Any of your delectable baked goods by chance?"

"Exactly my point. Besides, you best be getting out of here before Mr. Edwards gets home." Lillian started to close the door.

Oswald stepped halfway through to keep it open. "Why?" Oswald didn't like it when folks were upset with him, and the number of those who were seemed to be growing.

Lillian was already through her kitchen into the hallway beyond. She stopped and turned over her shoulder. "He said I should have seen your face. Looked like you wanted to kill that poor bird." She shook her head. "Make sure the door shuts on your way out—thanks." She disappeared into another room.

Oswald backed out of the door. It clicked shut. The sound echoed in his head and heart with the realization of how many of his friends were angry with him.

Surely this is just a misunderstanding. He was very fond of the Edwards. They'd saved him after his mother died. He wouldn't have survived otherwise. They took him in, sought the advice of local opossum experts, made him a nice nest in their garage, and fed him until he was old enough to fend for himself. That was when he moved in under Miss Ann's deck.

Oswald's heart beat faster and his paw pads were sweaty. He had that funny feeling in his stomach, like when he gave a speech—or rather like when he *thought* about giving a speech, as he hadn't given any yet. *I must speak to Joey—surely,* he *still likes me.*

Oswald checked the position of the sun—it was about one o'clock. Joey wouldn't be home yet. *Fiddle.* By now he'd missed his mid- and late-morning naps and he was ravenous. He walked down Perry Street and turned through the alley to Rhode Island Avenue. If he was lucky, there would be late lunchers and he could find some scraps.

Perfect. A woman in heels and a suit hurrying to her car dropped three fat French fries, still warm.

"Look at the size of that rat," she gasped. The insult was softened by her dropping her entire lunch. Stuffed to the gills, Oswald napped in a tree, setting his internal alarm for three thirty.

Joey sat on the front porch and jiggled his leg. His overnight backpack, stuffed to the max, was on the floor next to his feet. His mother stood over him. Having overslept, Oswald had rushed over to Joey's. When he heard him and Miss Ann on the porch, he slid into the overgrown lilac bush at the side. He peered over the edge, able to watch without being seen.

"This is for the best, Joey. If I catch you playing with that possum—"

"Oswald. His name is Oswald." Joey crossed his arms and looked away from his mother.

She pulled the other chair up and sat down. She tried to take both of Joey's hands in hers, which he didn't seem to want. Miss Ann laughed and settled on holding one. He made a face.

"I'm putting down the law, Joey. No contact with Oswald or you lose all computer privileges for three days—each time."

"But my biology project is due this Wednesday, and he was helping me with it, the 'Tale of Tails'. It's really cool, about all kinds of tails, like his, and the kangaroo's, and—"

"ENOUGH," Miss Ann said. Oswald flinched and dropped down into the overgrowth.

Joey clammed up. Miss Ann took a deep breath. "There's no school tomorrow—teacher training day. You get a long weekend over at your dad's. Isn't that nice?" She looked at her watch. "He'll be here any minute."

Joey grunted.

"Come on. You'll have fun with them over there. I'll pick you up on Sunday. We could stop by the animal rescue place where Naja is. Would you like that?"

Joey must have nodded because, after a beat, Miss Ann said, "Good. We'll do that. You might get more ideas for your school project. And I'm sure your dad can help you, too. And don't forget next Sunday a few folks, including Ria and her mom, are coming over for a barbeque. You like Ria, don't you?"

Oswald thought there was an awful lot planned. This wouldn't leave enough time for all the things he and Joey usually did together.

"She's OK."

"Joey, honey, it's nobody's fault Bradyn's dad got a job in Chicago."

There was a moment of quiet, except for two squirrels chasing and yammering at each other in a tree: "My tree. No, MY tree. No, MY tree. Nope, MY TREE. . ."

"I know you're shy, boo. It's OK, you'll make more friends."

"It's hard, Mom. I never know what to say. Kids invite me to play kickball and stuff, but sometimes I freeze. I don't know why. What if I never make any more friends?"

Oswald's heart sank. It took all his self-control not to jump up and tell him how smart and fun and interesting he was. This was exactly why Joey needed him in his life, and why his mother's meddling made no sense. Oswald couldn't help but sigh—a great heaving one that luckily coincided with Miss Ann sighing, too.

"You're just naturally shy, Joey. Everyone's different. We'll figure this out. I promise," she said.

"Promise?" Joey's voice was shaky.

"You bet. Hey—shy kids make great grown-ups. Did you know that?"

A car pulled up in front of the house. Chairs scraped, and Oswald heard the rustle of Joey's backpack heaving onto his shoulders.

"Give me a minute with your dad, OK?"

Oswald waited to hear her walk down the steps, then hoisted himself onto the porch.

"Psst, Joey, over here."

Joey startled out of a sullen stare. "You gotta get out of here. I'm going to lose computer privileges. Seriously."

"Yes, yes. I heard all that. Just nod or shake your head— that's not talking, is it?" Oswald said.

Joey nodded while keeping an eye on his mom and dad talking by the car.

"You still like me, right? I mean, I'm not so bad, am I?" Oswald said.

Joey shrugged. "Sometimes, it seems like you think you're better than everybody," he whispered out of the side of his mouth. "And sometimes you don't know when to stop talking."

Oswald was taken aback, but didn't have time to explain to Joey that he was just keeping everyone's standards high, challenging them to be their best selves.

Instead he cut to the chase. "Everyone seems to think I wanted to hurt that goose."

"Naja," Joey broke his code of silence again. "You did look fierce."

Oswald saw a sadness in Joey's eyes and remembered something else he wanted to say. "Joey, you're a terrific human, my favorite, as a matter of fact. You mustn't forget that. Ever. Will you give me your word?"

Joey looked at Oswald as though he didn't know what he was talking about, when footsteps approached the porch. Joey stood up and Oswald jumped off the side. Oswald scuttled around the corner to the front of the house, keeping cover under the shrubs—Miss Ann's neglected garden came in handy.

Joey's dad, Carlton, and Miss Ann stood at the bottom of the porch steps.

"Hey, Joey. You ready?" Carlton said. Oswald saw him quite a lot, although they hadn't been introduced. He stopped over once or twice a week and took Joey places. Joey said they usually went back to his dad's house in Upper Marlboro. Carlton lived with his wife Suzette and their two kids. Joey had his own room. "They have a pool and everything," Joey told him. It was often at that point that Oswald couldn't bear to hear anymore. Melvin knew all about Joey's dad, stepmom, and stepbrother and sister, and thought Oswald was jealous. Oswald thought that was ridiculous. He was sure no one was more important to Joey than Melvin, his mom, and of course him.

15

AN AIM AND A PURPOSE

For the first time since his mother died, Oswald didn't know what to do. He'd had lots of plans for the weekend, but now with Joey, Melvin, Zola, and the Edwards not talking to him, his plans sank like pebbles in a pond.

Oswald walked down Perry Street, stopped, turned around, and walked the other way. He walked and turned, walked and turned, until he was pacing in front of a house where some young guys called roofers were working. This seemed to be a type of human who climbed onto the tops of houses with no hesitation or fear. Sometimes they sat on top of the roof eating sandwiches or laying in the sun. They were loud and boisterous and with the way they climbed, these roofers reminded Oswald of raccoons.

The raccoons! They would know what to do. This thought gave Oswald the possibility of some company and help, as well as an aim and a purpose. And he always felt better with an aim and a purpose.

After a number of failed tries to cross Eastern Avenue, he remembered to go to the corner with the signaling device. He waited for some people to cross at the same time because he couldn't remember which of the three lights stopped the traffic.

Oswald turned left on Randolph Street NE. It looked wide as a river with trees lining both sides. There was a narrow path worn along the park; it was soft and warm on his paws. The smell of green grass was rich and comforting. He felt better already.

This is splendid. We can all go for a garbage buffet tonight. He saw a big tree with a hole halfway up and couldn't believe his luck. He climbed up to say hello, but found another opossum in it instead.

"So sorry. My mistake. You don't happen to know the raccoons, Tiny, Mo, and Chuck? They live in a big tree with a hole in it, much like yours?"

"Sorry, can't say I do," the other possum said. She gestured across the park. "There are lots of trees with good nesting holes."

Indeed there were. As this patch of earth turned away from the sun, Oswald realized this was going to be a lot harder than he thought.

He spent the rest of Thursday and into the night searching the many trees with dens. Nighttime was a bustling animal world. Possums, other raccoons, skunks, rats, mice, and house cats who liked to wander on the wild side filled the park. It was like rush hour on four paws. Darnell was right—there were plenty of animals in the park.

Oswald got turned around more than once and went in a few circles. He thought he'd ask someone about the basic layout and shape of the park. This would help him navigate. He approached an orange-and-white cat. He reasoned a pet who comes to the park must know enough to get home.

"The shape of the park?" she said. "Something like a triangle."

"Equilateral, isosceles, or scalene?"

"Show off." The cat flicked her tail and turned away.

"I was merely trying to clarify."

The cat huffed.

"Oh dear, oh dear," Oswald said. He bit his front claws, a habit he'd picked up from Joey. "I only aim to elucidate and communicate, never alienate. I want us all to collaborate and cooperate and—"

The cat turned toward Oswald. "Do you ever listen to yourself?" she said, then disappeared into the dense thicket.

"Oh dear, oh my. Now I'm offending beings I've just met." He realized he'd moved on to biting his back toenails and stopped.

As he continued his search, he was chased by dogs, was told off for having a quick nap in another possum's tree, and didn't find much food. With all the customers, the garbage buffets were emptied before Oswald figured out where they were. He found a good pizza crust with sauce on it, but a rat ran by and nabbed it right out of his paw.

Pizza. That's right! The raccoons stop at Twenty-Second Street Pizza every night.

16

THE KINDNESS OF STRANGERS

It took Oswald until nine o'clock the next morning to find the pizza place. But by then it was too late. No one was there, not the raccoons, not other animals, nor any humans. He decided to wait, not wanting to risk missing them again. Ravenous, he resorted to eating earthworms, like his mother taught him. He hated eating food that moved.

What if I never find Tiny, Mo, and Chuck? What if Joey and Miss Ann don't let me move back home?

At least, no matter what happened, he'd still have his writing career. Maybe he'd branch out from poetry. *Everything is material for a writer,* Oswald thought. *Yes, after this, I could write a survival guide for possums.* The Suburban Opossum's Guide to Living in City Parks. *I think there could be a good market for that!*

Having explored all sides of the building, Oswald thought his friends were most likely to come to the front. For one thing, there was a nice large wire trashcan. It was easy to climb up and into, and it didn't have a lid. Starting at lunchtime and into the evening, people kept tossing their crusts into it. Before he realized it, he had scaled the trashcan and was climbing in toward the sumptuous scraps. As he did, two teenaged girls emerged from the pizza parlor, each holding a hot slice. They chatted away, pausing to take bites.

"Good evening, young ladies. Let me introduce myself. I'm Oswald the opossum, and I was wondering if either of you might be so kind as to save me a bite of your pizza? Possibly some with cheese and sauce on it?" Oswald said as he wobbled on the rim.

One girl gave a long, high scream. Oswald fell to the ground. He was beginning to appreciate how rare Joey's talent for speaking Animal was.

A man with a white apron rushed out of the shop holding a baseball bat. "Everyone all right? What's going on?"

"You've got rats. Huge ones," the girl squeaked and pointed.

The man lowered his arm and chuckled. "That's just a possum." But it was too late. The sight of the large man with a bat made Oswald faint. The last thing he remembered was someone grabbing him by the base of his tail and tossing him into the trash can, but he was too far gone to do anything about his proximity to all those crusts. *What a waste.*

Oswald opened his eyes to a small slice of the night sky. He was warm and cozy with lots of stuff around him—paper, empty soda cans, crumpled paper napkins. He could smell himself—he must have fainted and let off that rotten smell. How embarrassing. He was often confused and befuddled after a faint. Then it started to come back to him—everyone shunning him at home, coming to the park to look for the raccoons, eating worms, and waiting for his friends at the pizza place.

Then he remembered the pizza man laughing, wielding a baseball bat. In his memory it looked like a scene from a horror movie. He wondered how badly he'd been beaten. *Odd, nothing hurts—I must be in shock.*

"Hey, it stinks here. Let's skip it," a voice said.

"When did smells ever stop us?" a sweeter voice said.

Oswald roused from his thoughts. "Help. Please, help! Someone? Anyone?" Oswald said.

The owner of the first voice scampered up the outside of the wire-mesh trashcan.

"Did you hear something?" the second, sweeter voice said from the ground.

Oswald looked through the wire mesh; there were two shiny eyes above a pointy nose and below small round ears.

"Aghh!" said the owner of the eyes before leaping down. Oswald could see him; it was a rat, who scampered over to another rat.

"Oh, don't be silly," the second rat said. "It's another critter. Maybe they're stuck." She climbed up the side until her face was level with Oswald's.

"Hi. I'm Tessa and that's Reginald, but everyone calls him Reggie. Are you all right?" she asked.

"I don't know. I don't think I can move."

"Have you tried?" Tessa said.

"I've been attacked. Who knows what injuries I've sustained? I thought it best not to move."

"Oh," Tessa said and blinked. "Well, if you don't mind, I see some nice pizza crusts in there."

"Of course. Be my guest," Oswald said. Reggie was already scampering in and out of the trashcan, making a series of clicks and whistles as he went. Tessa took things from Reggie and tossed them to the ground. A pile of pizza crusts grew, along with a few bottle tops and a broken shoelace.

"Wow, that looks like a lovely piece of tin foil under your back leg, Mr. . . . um, Mr. Possum. Would you mind?" Reggie said then made a few more clicks, apparently with his teeth.

"Oh, yes—I'm sorry. I'm Oswald, the opossum of Perry Street," Oswald said while handing Reggie the tin foil.

"Look! Your leg is working—that's great!" Tessa said.

Oswald looked at his back leg holding the tin foil as though it wasn't his. "Oh my, you're right," he said tentatively.

Reggie popped his head out from the trash gripping a plastic food container between his teeth. "Look at this, Tessa," Reggie said.

"Oh, Reggie. What will you do with that? We already have three."

Yet Reggie seemed to be on a mission. He grabbed one edge with his teeth and tried to climb up the inside of the wire mesh. But the plastic box was bigger than he was, and the rat and box dropped back onto the heaped garbage.

"Here. Maybe I can be of some assistance," Oswald wrapped his tail around the box and climbed up to the rim of the trashcan before he realized what he'd done. Reggie and Tessa climbed up with him clicking and cheering.

"Whoa," Oswald said as he balanced on the rim. The box dropped from his tail to the ground. "I'm feeling rather dizzy."

"Easy does it there, buddy," Reggie said. "Take my tail." He waved it in Oswald's direction. Oswald took it in his back paw. "Now what do I do?"

"Climb down backward," Tessa said. "That's it—take it slow," she reassured.

When they reached the ground, the rats cheered again, and Oswald fought tears of relief and embarrassment.

"What's the matter?" was all Tessa had to say, and Oswald cried in earnest. Oswald told them his story between splutters and tears. Tessa dabbed at his tears with her tail. But Reggie couldn't stay still. He went in and out of the trashcan, adding more things to their pile on the ground.

"Would you like to come with us? We make the rounds to a number of spots," Tessa offered.

"Oh, that's very kind, but I best wait here for my raccoon friends, Tiny, Mo, and Chuck," Oswald said. "They come every night."

Reggie skittered up to them after adding another scrap to the collection. "Do they have black masks?"

"I think they all have black masks," Oswald said.

"Yes, yes, now that you mention it," Reggie said as he arranged another pizza crust in his collection.

"I think we've met them here at the pizza place. Tiny's the big one? And Chuck's missing a chunk from his ear?" Tessa said.

"Yes, those are they!" Oswald said.

"If we see them, we'll certainly tell them you're waiting for them. Otherwise, if you're feeling all right now, we'll be on our way," Tessa said. "If we stay too long, Reggie won't be able to leave his collection."

"You're not taking those items with you?" Oswald said, eyeing the pizza crusts lined up.

"Oh, no—the fun's in the collecting. You're welcome to it," Reggie said as he scampered away from the pizza parlor with Tessa at his side.

Oswald called out. "Reggie? Tessa?" They stopped and turned around, eyes bright and whiskers wiggling under the streetlight.

"Yes?" Reggie said.

"Thank you. You've been ever so kind to a complete stranger." Oswald was mortified at having ever felt unkindly toward rats before. He made a silent promise to himself that if anyone ever mistook him for a rat again, he would simply say, "Thank you."

"No problem," Reggie said and made more clicks.

"Anytime," Tessa added.

The two rats turned and scampered out of the reach of the streetlights, and with their disappearing silhouettes came the realization that Oswald might never find the raccoons, might never be welcome back at Joey's, and might have to make a new life here by himself.

17

MISTAKEN IDENTITY

Oswald thought he would try to find Tiny, Mo, and Chuck one more time, by waiting out the night at the pizzeria. The hours after midnight and before dawn dragged. A few other animals came to check the trashcan. But so far, not his raccoon friends. Oswald passed the time eating the good things the rats had left behind. The sky was just promising to lighten when Oswald saw a large brown fur figure lumbering toward him.

"Mo!" Oswald rushed up to him, relieved to have finally found at least one of his friends. "I'm so glad to see you! Where are the others? I hope you don't mind, but I—"

"Oh, Grapejuice! You've come back!" The large brown animal wasn't Mo. She clamped Oswald in a hug.

"I'm ever so sorry, madam. I've mistaken you for someone else," Oswald said with some difficulty, given how tightly this critter was holding him.

"You always were a stitch." She laughed with her head back, releasing one paw long enough to slap her own side, before clasping it around Oswald again.

"No, really—I'm not who you think I am," Oswald tried again as she dragged him away from the pizza place. He pulled his head away as best he could to get a better look. "Are you a groundhog?" She sure looked like one, a big one at that, bigger than Oswald, maybe even as big as Tiny.

She tightened her vise-like hug. "Oh, how I missed you, dearie pie. Don't worry. We'll be home soon." Oswald tried to wiggle out but couldn't. The mammoth groundhog giggled. "You always were a snuggly one."

"Truly, madam. There's been some mistake."

She stopped, pinned him on his back to the earth. She gnashed her impressive incisors inches from his face and blinked her unfocused eyes. "You *bet* there's been some mistake—you *leaving me* was the mistake!" Then she picked him up with one paw, brushed him off with the other and continued the forced march. Her short, thick claws pressed through Oswald's fur and into his skin, stopping just before piercing it. Her voice was sweet as syrup, "But that's over now, isn't it, dearie pie?"

Surely she'll realize her mistake as soon as the sun comes up. Fighting her seemed pointless, and he didn't want to upset her further.

Dawn finally made good on its promise this Saturday morning. The animal rush hour was in full swing as the nocturnal shift made its way back to their nests.

"Good morning. How are you?" Oswald greeted the various animals they passed hoping for any chance for intervention. They mostly nodded and scurried on, especially, it seemed, once they saw this groundhog's face.

Then he saw a wonderful sight. Reggie and Tessa were walking with the three raccoons. They were all chatting away as they strolled in the other direction, back toward the pizza parlor.

"Reggie, Tessa! Tiny, Mo, Chuck! What a wonderful surprise!" Oswald could feel the groundhog's grip tighten.

The rats and raccoons snapped their heads around and looked at the unlikely duo.

"Oh, you left the pizzeria. We bumped into the raccoons and were just going back that way with them. Reggie really wants that plastic box." Tessa rolled her eyes.

"Hi, Oswald, why don't you introduce us to your girl-friend." Chuck beamed.

"Girlfriend? You have a *girlfriend*, do you? And why are they calling you 'Oswald'?" the groundhog said in a high-pitched chirp that didn't match her size. She gave a quick sob without loosening her grip.

"Help," Oswald gasped.

Tiny stepped forward. "Hello, madam. I'm Tiny. Do you know our friend Oswald?"

She gave a dramatic sigh. "You're breaking my heart. Are you telling me he has another identity? My Grapejuice has an-other life? My sister warned me about this!" She held Oswald away from her like a rag doll, stared at him with glazed eyes, then clamped him back to her side. "Don't worry, dearie pie. All is forgiven—you've come back to me now." Another sob stuttered out of her.

"Oh, no, madam." Reggie stood on his hind legs, his long tail balancing him. "That's Oswald. He's an opossum."

"Don't be ridiculous! What sort of fool do you take me for? Friends of his, I bet. In cahoots with him and his meandering ways!"

"I'm Tessa. What's your name?" Tessa said stepping for-ward. "I can't imagine what it's like to lose your husband—"

"I didn't *lose* him. He's not a set of keys, or an acorn. He *left* me." The groundhog leaned down into Tessa's face with-out loosening her grasp. Her incisors were much longer than Tessa's. "I'm Pixie, thanks for asking." She straightened up.

"Nice to meet you, Pixie," Tessa's voice quavered. "But please understand. The fellow you have there isn't your hus-band Grapejuice."

"Don't you think I'd know my husband when I see him?" She glared with unfocused eyes inches from Oswald. "OK, well, I certainly recognize his wonderful scent, like a wet woolen mitten."

They were all quiet for a moment. Then Tessa tried again, "We all make mistakes, Pixie . . . isn't that right, guys?" The other animals nodded and made soft noises of agreement.

Pixie squeezed him harder. He gasped for breath. "Oh, you think you all know so much. Well, if this isn't Grapejuice—prove it!" She gnashed her teeth.

Reggie stepped forward and put a paw around Tessa. "How?"

Pixie stood her full height, lifting Oswald off the ground. "If this isn't Grapejuice, then you go find him and bring him back to me. We'll be home." She nodded toward the opening to a large burrow in the roots of a bigger tree. "We'll be right there, won't we, dearie pie?" Oswald squeaked for air again.

18

FLOCK DISORDER

"Don't slam the door," Miss Ann said, sitting in the car as Joey got in.

"I didn't," Joey said.

His mother started the car and waved at Joey's stepmom, Suzette, on the steps of a rectangular house with the lawn mowed in stripes. Joey's dad, Carlton, washed his car in the driveway. He smiled and waved.

Joey's half-siblings, Mary, six, and Noah, four, ran around on the grass. Noah flapped his arms while looking at Joey.

"You did *not* tell that child he could fly, did you?" Miss Ann said.

"I don't know. Maybe."

"You are *not* still mad about the 'no possum' rule, are you?"

"I don't know. Maybe."

Ann drove out of the neighborhood and onto Route 301 North. She turned the radio on. Joey turned it off and the air conditioning up.

"OK, so you *do* want to talk?"

"Nope."

"Well, did you have a nice time at your dad's over the weekend?"

"Yeah. It was OK," Joey said and stopped hunching his shoulders.

They drove through another patch of quiet. The tires hummed against the asphalt.

"Remember when you learned this road was called Blue Star Memorial Highway and you wanted to know who killed the blue star?" his mother said.

"I was little then." He stared out the window.

"Well, I thought it was cute, and I still think you're cute. Even if you're not talking to me."

Thick rows of trees lined the road like they were waiting to take over. They gave way to a few stores and a traffic light. Miss Ann turned right. After passing Fredrick Douglass High School, the road got more countrified: fields, barns, woods, and more fields.

"Where are we going?" Joey said.

"Merkle Wildlife Sanctuary. Remember? I said we'd go see how Naja's doing."

"I don't get it. You don't want me talking to animals, then you take me someplace where there's loads of them?"

They passed a few houses and she turned left. "I think your talent with animals is great. Maybe you'll be a vet when you grow up." They passed a few historic-looking brick buildings and a church. "When you're in high school, you could try to get a job at a place like this."

Joey stopped slumping. "You can get paid for hanging out with animals?"

"You know that. You go to the vet when we bring Melvin, and you've seen Animal Control in action—"

"Animal Control stinks."

They turned at a sign painted with Canada geese and the words *Merkle Wildlife Sanctuary*. Fields of tall sun-tired grass stretched out before them. Trees edged the left, and to the right at a distance was the Patuxent River. There were streams and marshy areas closer in. They passed a pole with a wooden box at the top, brimming with twigs and grass. A peregrine falcon eyed them.

His mother parked next to a cinder block building. There was a truck and a van out front with the center's insignia on the sides.

It was as hot as a pizza oven. Miss Ann pressed the doorbell, and Ms. Harris, the woman who had taken Naja from their house, came out.

"Hi, Ms. Jones, Joey. Glad you could come on my shift." Her badge read *Barbara Harris*. "Follow me, it's a bit of a walk." She had a camera around her neck.

"What's the camera for, Ms. Harris?" Joey asked as they continued on wooden walkways above sodden, marshy ground. A rich smell of green gave way to the aroma of swamp. Joey and Miss Ann slapped at hungry mosquitoes. Ms. Harris must have had on bug spray—they left her alone.

"We'd like a few pictures of Naja with her rescuers for our website, if that's OK?" Ms. Harris said.

"Of course," Ann responded. Ms. Harris stopped in front of a wooden building on the edge of a finger of the river. A sign on the door read *Flock Disorder—Infirmary*.

"What's flock disorder, Ms. Harris?" Joey said.

"Some of these mixed-breed birds have trouble fitting in with a flock. Their looks or behaviors are just that much different. The other birds don't recognize them as one of their own—don't let them join. Sometimes they never find a flock. That's difficult for social animals like these." Ms. Harris unlocked the door and swung it open. "Come on in."

It was cool, dim, and quiet inside. There were four pens with wire mesh tops, each with a wading pool, bedding, and food and water. One label read *Mute + Trumpeter Swan*.

"Poor thing makes a sound and is surprised each time," Ms. Harris said.

Other labels read: *Buff + American Blue Goose,* and *Mallard + American Black Duck.*

"Are they"—Joey looked around and lowered his voice—"a little dumb or something? Is that why they don't fit in?"

Ms. Harris stood in front of the fourth pen. "No, often it's quite the opposite. You tend to get better, smarter, stronger animals when you mix up the genes."

"Really?" Joey stopped in his tracks and looked up at Ms. Harris.

"Yes, a lot of the time it works that way. There's a term for it, 'hybrid vigor.'"

Joey grinned. "Then I must be brilliant *and* super strong because I'm one-eighth Piscataway Native American, one-sixteenth Chinese, one-quarter—"

"OK, Mr. Wikipedia," Miss Ann said. "I'm sure Ms. Harris has better things to do besides listen to you carry on."

Ms. Harris laughed. She opened the gate to the fourth pen. "That's OK, Ms. Jones. It's great when kids are interested. I have plenty of info about hybrid vigor if you want to stop by my office later."

Joey looked at his mom. "Maybe I could do my science project on it."

"If you're sure?" Miss Ann said to Ms. Harris.

"Of course. But first, I think Naja could do with a visit." She stepped away from the opened pen.

There she was, a feathered mass on the floor. She had one wing bandaged to her body, her head tucked under the other, a bit of a pink foot visible. Her body expanded and slumped as if in a sigh.

"Naja, what's the matter?" Joey stepped forward. The bird heaved another sigh but kept her head under her wing.

"Go on in. Maybe you two can cheer her up. She's been depressed and hasn't been eating much."

Miss Ann put her hand on Joey's shoulder and drew him back. "Let me go first." Joey was surprised to see tears in her eyes. She crouched down and stroked Naja's back. She started to sing the same lullaby she sang to her after she crashed onto their roof. After a few notes, Naja ruffled her feathers and took her head out. When she saw Miss Ann, she gave a long, sad sound then draped her long black-feathered neck across Miss Ann's shoulder.

When she got to the end of the song, Naja spoke in quick, urgent tones. Joey looked up at Ms. Harris and then his mother.

"Is it true? She'll never fly again?"

19

SEEING CLEARLY

"I don't understand. Why are you all lying to me, saying this isn't Grapejuice?" Pixie made some chirping sounds and blinked at Tiny and Tessa, who sat across from her in her den. It was a nice size, with packed earth walls and floor. There was a grass bed, a piece of wood for a table, and cubbyholes carved into the walls with seeds and dried plants in them. You could see two spots on the wall where pictures used to hang. It smelled clean and earthy. Oswald was pinned under Pixie, her four sturdy paws gripping his.

"Everything all right down there?" Mo's voice came in, along with the shaft of sunlight through the entrance hole. They all looked up—as much as they could, in Oswald's case.

"We're just having a chat," Tiny said.

"A chat?" Pixie said, her mood brightening. "Well, it is nice to have company. But I'm afraid I don't have anything to offer you. So, if you've stopped your silliness, it's probably best you all go and give us some privacy."

"No!" Oswald managed. "Please don't go, good fellows . . . and gal."

"Don't worry," Tessa whispered to him.

"Has Chuck or Reggie found anyone that might help, yet?" Tiny called upward.

There were other voices mixed in with Mo's when he called down, "Ms. Pixie, we found two friends of yours, Esmeralda and Simone. All right if they come down?"

"That's great—yes, they know Grapejuice. They'll tell you it's him," Pixie said.

The nose of another opossum poked through the hole and hovered, then the whole possum scrabbled down. She nodded "hello" to everyone, then scooted next to Tessa.

"Hi, Esmeralda," Pixie said. She lifted one front paw and nodded toward her captive. "Look, Grapejuice is back—isn't that wonderful?"

"Um, well . . . ," Esmeralda said.

"Hold on, I'm coming," came from the opening, then the sounds of someone else sliding down.

Oswald craned his neck—*a skunk!* "Please don't spray us," he yelped from under Pixie. Tiny and Tessa's eyes were big. Tessa started for the exit.

"Don't worry. Of course I won't spray," the skunk said.

The new possum nodded. "That's right. Simone has good control."

"I'm sorry, I forgot to introduce myself. I'm Simone. I've lived next door to Pixie, well, since I can remember. Please stay," she said to Tiny and Tessa. "What's going on?"

"Oh, Simone. I'm so glad to see you. Tell these critters that this *is* Grapejuice! I don't know why they won't believe us, why they want to ruin our happiness—isn't that right, dearie pie?" She gave a quick sob into her shoulder without loosening her grip. Oswald made a muffled sound. Tiny reached forward and extended a paw toward Oswald. Pixie gnashed her teeth aggressively in his direction. "See what I mean?"

Oswald pushed his snout out a bit to see better. Pixie didn't seem to notice. Simone looked at Tiny and Tessa then back toward Pixie with a very gentle expression.

"Pixie, we know how hard this has been on you—Grapejuice up and leaving like that—" Simone started. Esmeralda nodded.

Pixie let out a wail. "You have no idea. He was the green in my grass, the warmth in my fur . . . " She trailed off.

Esmeralda stepped up to Pixie and rested her head on Pixie's shoulder. "Don't be sad." Pixie took her front paws off Oswald and hugged Esmeralda back. Tiny dove under her and grabbed Oswald by his outstretched forelimbs. Pixie swayed backward as Tiny pulled Oswald free. Pixie fell on her bottom, still hugging Esmeralda. Everyone untangled into a circle of panting animals in Pixie's well-swept den.

Simone was the first to speak. "Let's find your glasses, Pixie. Remember, the ones your sister bought you for your birthday?"

"What? Those? They make me look fat . . . and buck-toothed. They're no good. I keep them in the cubbyhole, be-hind the nuts for when my sister comes around, but I don't know why you want me to—"

Simone gestured over her shoulder, then nodded to Tessa who immediately climbed on top of Simone, stretched up-ward, and dug in the first, then the second cubbyhole.

"Found them!" Tessa balanced on top of Simone's shoul-der, waving a pair of sparkly eyeglasses above her head. Tiny took them from her and offered them to Pixie.

"If y'all insist. I still don't see the point . . . " She put the glasses on and stared gape-mouthed. "Why, Esmeralda, who's this other possum? Is it your brother?"

After another hard sob, Pixie couldn't apologize enough. "I'm so sorry. I'm mortified. I don't know what's got into me. Maybe I do need to wear these glasses after all." She smiled a toothy, embarrassed grin below her glasses, which were glint-ing in the shaft of sunlight.

"Ms. Pixie, I think if anyone here understands, I do," Os-wald said. All animals' eyes turned toward him. "I know what it's like to want something so much it clouds your thinking."

The animals were quiet, waiting for Oswald to continue. He stretched from his confinement, shaking out his limbs. "I'm sorry Grapejuice let you down, Ms. Pixie. There's someone I don't want to let down—a really nice boy named Joey Jones. I'm supposed to go to his school on Wednesday and help him with his project. But now, well, everything's gone wrong. And it's all my fault."

He fell silent as he looked up the light-filled exit, as though it were an impossible climb from where he was to where he needed to be.

20

HOMEWARD BOUND

"I think that's plenty, Joey," Ms. Harris said. She looked over his shoulder at the computer he was working on at her desk. There were stacks of papers everywhere, a cup filled with large feathers, and a walkie-talkie she used to talk to other center staff.

"You think?" But he didn't wait for Ms. Harris to respond; he was unable *not* to talk about his project due tomorrow. "OK. So, I'll start by explaining what hybrid vigor is, also called *het-er-o-sis,* and why mixing up genes can make animals stronger. How if there's a bad gene—one that makes a problem—it's more likely to be sort of covered up by another good one. And how having different genes for the immune system makes you better at fighting diseases. And how mules are a *really* good example of this because they're *much* stronger than horses or donkeys, their parents . . . " Joey paused to take a breath and clicked to a chart about how much mules, horses, elephants, and camels could carry.

Joey turned to look up at Ms. Harris. "Wow, mules can carry *three times* as much as horses? And they're stronger than camels, too. Why doesn't everyone use mules?"

Ms. Harris laughed. "That's a good question, Joey. Maybe there are some ways horses are better. I don't know. But it could come down to belief. Belief is often stronger than fact—"

"That's weird, Melvin always says that."

"Melvin?"

"Yeah, my cat."

"Of course."

The door opened, and Miss Ann walked in with a male staff member. "It's all set, Barbara. We'll set up the pool and pen at the Joneses' tomorrow then bring Naja over on Thursday," he said.

"We're getting a pool?" Joey said.

"It's for Naja, boo," Miss Ann said. "That will be one of your jobs, keeping kids out. It's not very big—like a wading pool."

Joey turned back to the computer and crossed his arms. "Great. Another way to be popular—get a pool no one can go in."

"Someone's still mad about the no-possum rule," his mother said to Ms. Harris.

"You know, Joey, you'll have to take over for us. Helping Naja exercise. Give her the best chance of flying again." Ms. Harris leaned across Joey and pressed keys on the computer.

"She *will* be able to fly again, right?" Joey said.

Ms. Harris fiddled with the computer, then handed Joey a computer flash drive. "You just never know with these things. Sometimes birds recover fully from even the most terrible fractures to their wings, and other times, even the smallest crack never heals right. We'll have to wait and see. But going home with you guys is the best thing for her. She won't have to see all these other geese flying around. We think that's what's depressing her. Plus, Naja's really bonded with your mom."

"I guess," Joey said, looking rather glum.

"You guess what, young man?" Miss Ann said.

"I guess I can help Naja. And I guess I can share my mom with a goose."

21

CARTOON BLUE SKY

It was a glorious May morning on Wednesday, with a cartoon blue sky. There was no wind—like the world was holding its breath. Animals gathered under, and on, the raccoons' tree. There were the rats, Reggie and Tessa; Simone, the skunk; and Esmeralda, the opossum. The orange-and-white cat Oswald had met in the park came, after Tiny convinced her Oswald was a nice guy underneath. Her name was Queenie. There were two squirrels—or maybe there were three. It was hard to tell because they kept chasing each other around the tree. A crow named Frank waited on a low branch. And of course, there were the raccoons, Tiny, Mo, and Chuck.

Some of the animals yawned and stretched, struggling to stay awake, as this was their normal bedtime. Tiny ambled up to the front of the crowd. Oswald sat next to him.

"Thank you, everyone, for participating in this exciting animal-human event," Tiny said. "We will be helping a Mr. Joseph Carlton Jones, human, aged ten, in his biology class today. Now I turn you over to our director, Oswald, the opossum of Perry Street." There was a round of paws applause. Oswald was surprised at how nervous he was. *I need to get used to public speaking—fame will have its demands.* He stared at the small crowd, wrapping and unwrapping his tail around his front leg—that nervous habit of his.

"Psst. Oz," Chuck whispered from the sidelines.

Oswald shook his head as though coming out of a dream. "Yes, yes. First I want to thank all of you for your generosity and hospitality over these past few days. I am grateful for your help as we push the boundaries of animal-human relations. With this project, we will march into the future and leave the past behind, which will place us squarely in a new present, which used to be our future, and will soon be our past—"

Tiny bustled up and clapped his paw on Oswald's back. "Thank you, Oswald, for that inspiring speech. A big round of applause for our director, Mr. Oswald."

Oswald bowed at the applause but was confused. He hadn't realized he'd finished.

"Please, everyone, line up in the following order." Tiny slipped the clipboard made of a cup lid out of Oswald's clenched paw.

"Let's see . . . Reggie and Tessa, you're first, then the squirrels, followed by the opossum, Esmeralda." Tiny waited while these animals got in line.

"Next we have Chuck, to represent raccoon tails, then Queenie the cat, and last but not least, Simone Skunk. Mo, you'll take up the rear," Tiny continued.

"Oh, thanks—*behind* the skunk?" Mo said.

There was a bustling noise across the grass toward the tree. Pixie. "Don't worry—I wouldn't let you all down," she called out. She stopped next to Tiny and stood on her hind paws, panting. She had a dish towel wrapped around her with a twig stuck through as a fastener.

"Oh no," Mo said, not quite under his breath.

"What's with the towel?" Reggie said.

"I couldn't go *naked*. Not in front of all those children." Pixie smiled, her long front teeth twinkling along with her glasses.

The animals gave a collective groan.

"Naked? We're animals. We have fur, for Pete's sake—" Mo started.

Pixie batted her eyes. "Who's Pete? Introduce me!" She adjusted her towel, and tripped on it.

No one said anything for a moment. After Pixie had seen the truth and let Oswald go on Sunday, the animals had been working together to do the presentation at Joey's school today, like Oswald had promised. It turned out that most animals wanted to improve animal-human relations. There had been so many misunderstandings over the years.

But Pixie got on everyone's nerves. She was loud, interrupted all the time, and had a lot of goofy ideas. She made it hard to get anything done. They'd decided to do the school presentation without her and lied about when they were going—they'd told her it was this afternoon, rather than in the morning.

Although Oswald found her annoying at times, too, he also knew what it was like to be Pixie. He knew what it was like when everyone you cared about found you annoying and how sometimes you might not even realize it. He'd felt bad about lying to her to try to keep her from coming, but felt he couldn't go against everyone else's wishes. He stepped forward.

"That's lovely of you to help, Pixie. You can show the children how the fur on your tail stands on end when you're scared."

"Like mine," Queenie chimed in.

There was another round of groans from most of the other animals, but not as loud this time.

"Yes, why don't you line up behind Queenie, then?" Oswald said. Pixie grinned and loped to her place in line.

"Caw, caw. What about me?" Frank, the crow, said from his perch on the tree.

"You'll fly above us. We need your help crossing Eastern Avenue," Oswald said, then took the clipboard back from Tiny.

"Before we start, let's review our assignments one more time," Oswald said.

The group complained some more, but Oswald continued. "Reggie and Tessa, you will explain how rats use their tails to radiate heat and cool their bodies down when it's too hot. Remember to tell everyone this is why your tails are hairless."

"Right-ee-oh," Reggie and Tessa said. Reggie made clicking sounds.

Oswald alternated between looking up at the group and down at the clipboard. "So, those of you who use your tails for balance and keeping warm are the squirrels, skunk, raccoons, and Queenie. And communicating—we all use our tails for communicating, right? And one last thing, Esmeralda, don't forget to explain about our prehensile tails, how we can wrap our tails around things like branches."

But the animals had already started to move off, leaving the fragrant grass of the park and heading along Twenty-Fourth Street NE. They followed Tiny toward the left along the long stretch of Randolph Street. The few people they passed either said hello, even though they didn't seem to understand Animal, or were in too much of a rush to notice them. Tiny halted at the corner of Eastern Avenue where cars and trucks barreled by.

"I got this," Frank said. He perched on a telephone line and told them when it was safe to cross, saving them the time it would have taken to walk to the corner where the signaling device was.

After they crossed Eastern Avenue and walked into Mount Rainier, Oswald was hit with a wave of homesickness. This was his first time back there for six days, although it felt like much longer. Rhododendrons, azaleas, and dogwoods bloomed in front of the well-kept wooden bungalows and brick houses. Flowerpots, scooters, and bikes decorated front porches.

Oswald passed a bungalow that looked a lot like the Edwardses' except there wasn't a dog in the yard. *I wonder how Zola is. I bet Melvin's having his morning nap in the sun in the study right now.* And then one other thought: *What if Joey thinks I forgot about his school project?* That stopped him in his tracks, like a punch in the chest. He hadn't known that disappointing someone else, even only wondering if you had, could make you feel so awful.

Frank pulled Oswald's tail. "Come on. We better catch up." Frank flew toward the parade of animals scampering, waddling, and trotting ahead. They turned left. Oswald scurried to catch up. They were down to only one squirrel by then, Hazel. The others got distracted going up and down trees. Oswald was panting by the time he reached the front of the school where the animals waited for him.

He looked up the nine cement steps to the two wooden doors. The red brick building was a series of rectangular boxes stacked in three layers. Oswald remembered Joey telling him about "that awful first day at school feeling" he got every year and thought he might understand what Joey had been talking about, now. Eleven pairs of eyes looked at him.

"You go first, Oswald. This is your show," Tiny said.

"Yes, of course." Oswald climbed up, and the other animals followed. They were faced with a non-animal-friendly door. Chuck stood on Tiny's shoulders and used all his strength to open it enough to let them all dash in.

It was quiet, cool, and dim inside. It smelled like wood and cleaning fluid. The floor was cold. The walls were painted cinder block. There was a large glass case along one side with trophies and pictures of students. Ahead of them, they heard paper rustling, followed by a throat clearing.

"May I help you?" a man said. He sat at a desk. He wore a dark blue uniform with a badge on his shirt—*Mr. Robinson.* Joey had talked about him and said he was nice.

Oswald walked up to the desk and stood on his hind legs. Mr. Robinson peered over and frowned.

"Good morning, sir. I am the director of the Barnard Hill Animal Alliance"—this was what they had decided to call themselves—"We are here to assist Joseph Carlton Jones in his class presentation today."

"I'm sorry, I don't speak Animal. And I'm afraid we don't allow animals in without a human chaperone. Do you have one?"

Oswald didn't know what to say. He hadn't thought of this possibility. He stared and blinked.

Mr. Robinson sighed, scraped his chair back, and stood up. He nodded at each animal, as though he was counting. "You guys wait here. I'll be right back. I'll go try to find someone who speaks Animal."

22

A DOUBLE-DECKER RACCOON WITH A CROW ON TOP

"Go!" Tiny said.

"Aren't we supposed to wait for Mr. Robinson?" Oswald's voice echoed against the cinderblock walls. But it was useless. All the other animals were already hauling their feathered and furry butts down the hall after Tiny. Oswald charged after them to catch up.

There was a flapping clatter against a ceiling light, and Frank crashed to the floor.

"Get on my back—no good flying inside," Chuck said.

A woman came out of a classroom at the noise and peered over her glasses.

"Excuse me, madam, you look knowledgeable." Oswald thought it best to start with flattery. Do you know what class Joseph Jones, human, aged ten years, is in?"

The woman stared at Oswald, crossed her arms, and tapped her foot. *She must not speak Animal.* Children sat at desks behind her. They all had light-blue tops and navy-blue pants or skirts. Two held their hands in the air, straight up. *Was this a salute?* One girl with thick, dark wavy hair waved her hand at the back of the teacher's head.

"Joey Jones. He's in Ms. Tinderclaw's class upstairs," the girl said.

The teacher turned toward the girl, annoyed. "Thank you, Valeria, for *interpreting*."

"Upstairs—Joey's upstairs," Oswald called to the others.

"There, on the left," Mo hollered. The animals, with Frank flapping to keep balanced on Chuck's back, skidded and scrabbled to make the turn. Pixie's towel fell to the floor. Then, wham—a woman coming down the stairs with a large stack of files tripped over them. The woman shrieked as she tumbled down the stairs, files spilling everywhere.

Doors opened. Teachers rushed out. Two helped the woman up. Others gathered the files. Students peered out of the open doors.

Lots of voices said lots of things:

"Wow, are we having an assembly?"

"You all right?"

"I'm fine, just surprised."

"Someone call the front office."

"Don't worry, Animal Control's coming."

Already up the stairs, the critters bounded and loped as fast as they could. There were doors—so many doors—lining both sides of the hall.

"Oh, dear, oh my," Oswald said.

"Stop your whining," Mo said. "Tiny, come here, give Chuck a boost." Tiny hurried over. Chuck climbed on his shoulders, with Frank still balancing on his. Chuck knocked on the door. A man with short hair and a bow tie opened it.

"May I help you?" He didn't look surprised to be talking to a double-decker raccoon with a crow on top.

"Excuse me, Mr. Stazco," a voice said from behind the animals. It was Valeria, the girl from the classroom downstairs. "I've been sent from the front office to escort them." She waved a piece of paper, then clasped both hands and the paper behind her back. Mr. Stazco smiled and thanked her before closing the door.

"It's really a bathroom pass. Quick, follow me. I'll show you where Joey is."

"This is very kind of you, Valeria," Oswald said.

"Call me Ria. No problem. I kind of know Joey. Our moms are friends." She hurried down the hall, stopping at room 235.

"This is it." Ria ran back down the hall, her footsteps echoing and her long hair bouncing on her back.

An ear-splitting bell sounded, followed by a recorded voice from speakers on the ceiling: "This is an emergency. Please listen carefully for instructions." There was the sound of someone tapping on a microphone, then a man's voice.

"This is your principal, Mr. Grant. We have been infiltrated by a pack of unchaperoned animals. All pupils are to stay in their classrooms until the problem is contained. And do *not* touch the animals under any circumstances. Thank you."

"'Problem?' I don't like his attitude," Oswald said.

"Forget it, Oswald. We've only got a few minutes, if we have any chance of helping Joey," Tiny said.

Tiny walked up to the door and gave a loud rap. A woman opened it and made that human error of looking over their heads at first. When she saw them, she gasped and shoved the door closed, but Pixie had already positioned herself with her back against the doorjamb and her four paws against the door.

"Hurry, everybody in!" Pixie grunted with the strain. She showed her teeth and the teacher stepped back from the door. The animals scampered over Pixie and stood in a group at the front of the room. The teacher backed up against the wall next to the whiteboard. Her voice was shaky.

"Stay back, children. Do *not* touch them. They might have diseases." There were gasps across the room. Some stood up to see better.

Oswald climbed onto the large empty chair at the front. He looked across the sea of young, receptive faces. The children all wore those light-blue tops. He marveled at how the teacher could tell them apart: they had no striped fur on their faces and he couldn't see many of their ears; the ones he could see weren't much help in telling the kids apart. He looked at each one in turn. Then he saw Joey. He felt desperate and hopeful at the same time. He ran across the desks to him. "Don't touch the animals!" The teacher screeched.

"Joey, wonderful to see you!" Oswald said and snuggled up to him before he could stop himself.

"Aw, how cute," a girl said.

"Wow, Joey—you know all these animals?" a boy said.

"How'd you get them to do all this stuff?"

"How'd they know what room you were in?"

"How'd they get past Mr. Robinson?"

Lots of kids asked lots of questions.

"Class—quiet!" The teacher climbed on her wheeled chair, and moved it toward the door by moving her hands along the wall until reaching the phone.

"This is Ms. Tinderclaw in room 235. The animals Mr. Grant was talking about? They're in my room." There was a pause. "Yes . . . yes. . . . Well, I'm afraid Joseph Jones has had contact." Another short silence. "Yes, he did know. . . . Oh . . . OK . . . I will. Bye." Ms. Tinderclaw hung up and turned toward the class. "Joey, the animals have been asking for you—seems a girl in a class downstairs understands Animal, too. You will need to go down to the office after they're contained."

"I didn't have anything to do with this, Ms. Tinderclaw. Honest," Joey said, then he continued to Oswald in a whisper, although everyone could hear anyway.

"Oswald—what are you doing here? Who are all these guys?"

The rest of the animals stood at the front of the room.

"I'm Tiny, and these are our colleagues. We're here to demonstrate our tails for your project," Tiny said. He raised a front paw in the air and all the animals waved, wiggled, or waggled their tails.

A couple of students in the front row screamed and ran to the back of the room when they saw Simone put her tail straight up in the air and wave it.

"Apologies for any undue alarm," Tiny said. "Ms. Simone Skunk will *not* spray during the demonstration. We will start with our rat friends, Reggie and Tessa."

The animals demonstrated and explained about each of their tails, just like they had practiced. Joey, being the only other person in the school besides Ria who spoke Animal, translated for Ms. Tinderclaw and the other students. After a few minutes, Ms. Tinderclaw climbed down from her chair and sat on it. "There's no harm in listening to their presentation. Everyone, just stay calm while we wait for Animal Control."

Oswald was in the middle of his explanation of prehensile tails with Esmeralda, who curled and uncurled her tail around a ruler, when the door opened and two uniformed Animal Control officers came in, a man and a woman.

They were carrying transport cages. The woman interrupted Oswald.

"Good morning, children. We're Prince George's County Animal Control officers, and we've come to, um . . . ," the female officer said.

"We've come to escort these animals out," the male officer said.

"Excuse me, but I was in the middle of my report to these children. I'm sure you don't want to impede their education." *At least these people understand Animal.* Oswald crossed his front paws and tapped a back one. No one said anything for a moment. The clock on the wall ticked.

"Where's Mr. Darnell Anderson? He is my liaison to Animal Control."

"Your *liaison*?" the man asked.

The two officers looked at each other then the teacher, who shrugged indicating she didn't understand Animal. Oswald was glad to see them taking him seriously. The man spoke again.

"I'm afraid Mr. Anderson is not on duty today, but I assure you we can provide equally good service," the woman said. Then the man continued.

"We are very sorry to interrupt, but the school has a strict policy of no animal visitors without a human chaperone," the man said.

Oswald cleared his throat. "We are *not* leaving until we finish our presentation. This was an animal-human promise. And *we* keep our promises."

"What are they saying? What's going on? Joey, tell us." The kids asked for interpretation. The teacher looked curious, but didn't say anything.

"Later," Joey whispered back to them.

The woman officer spoke. "We talked to your principal, Mr. Grant, before coming up, and he said he would arrange an assembly where you could give your demonstration to a lot more children at once. That is, if you come with us now."

"I need to confer with my colleagues," Oswald said. The animals huddled for a moment before Oswald gave their answer. "We believe we can meet your demands *if* you can guarantee press coverage."

The male officer spluttered. The female one jabbed her elbow into his ribs. "I think we can arrange that," she said. "Let me step out into the hall and make a few calls."

"That's very decent of you," Oswald said. He trotted over to Joey's desk. The male officer eyeballed him but didn't say anything.

"Oh, Joey, this is terrific. It looks like it's all working out. I'll move back. Your mom will be delighted to have a celebrity living at her house," Oswald whispered.

Joey whispered back, "I don't know. There's lots going on at home right now, and then it's my mom's birthday on Sunday …" Joey trailed off, looked like he was concerned about something, then continued. "Hey, thanks for all this stuff about tails, but I didn't get a chance to tell you—I changed my topic to hybrid vigor—"

The female officer came back in the room, beaming. "Mr. Opossum—"

"Oswald. It's Oswald." He trotted back to the front of the room.

"Sorry, Mr. Oswald. You will be delighted to know that the *Washington Post* will send a reporter and photographer to cover the assembly whenever it's scheduled."

"That's excellent," Oswald said.

The officers put the cages on the floor with the doors open and let the animals decide how to divide themselves up. Oswald wanted a cage to himself, as the director and soon-to-be star, but was convinced to let Reggie and Tessa join him, as there weren't enough cages for him to have his own.

Joey was floating on air and adrenaline. He wasn't used to all this attention. It felt good, but also made him uncomfortable. He squinted in the sharp afternoon sun as he left school. Usually hardly anyone talked to him. But today, everyone wanted to say hi.

"Hey, Dr. Dolittle."

"Dude, that was really cool."

"I hear you can hypnotize animals. Can you show me?"

"Yeah, can you hypnotize my little sister?"

"Saw you come out of the principal's office. You in trouble?"

Joey answered everyone honestly, except for how much trouble he was in. He wasn't in any, but he left it vague. If they guessed he'd gotten some big punishment, he didn't want to "confuse them with the truth"—one of Mr. Edwards's sayings.

Mr. Grant believed Joey when he said he hadn't asked the animals to come. Luckily, Joey had given his presentation on hybrid vigor a few minutes before the animals showed up. Ms. Tinderclaw confirmed all this. In fact, Mr. Grant had to ask Joey to stop explaining how it wasn't his fault a few times before Joey would stop talking.

"We have to call your mom, Joey. Because you had physical contact with a wild animal—"

"That's Oswald, he's not wild, and if he wasn't feeling well, believe me—I'd hear more about it than I'd want to," Joey said before he could stop himself. Interrupting a grown-up was never a good idea, especially when it was your school principal. Joey gulped and gathered the courage to look at Mr. Grant to see how mad he was. But he wasn't. He looked like he was trying to hide a smile.

"Well, that may be, but we'll still need to tell your mother. Let her decide if you need any shots."

"But, sir, I'm *sure* it's Oswald. See, you can identify opossums by the patterns of black and white on their ears and forepaws—"

Mr. Grant checked his watch and stood up. "Mr. Jones, that's quite enough." He didn't look amused this time.

"Sorry, Mr. Grant." Joey suddenly realized he might have the same problem Oswald had—not quite knowing when to be quiet and listen.

23

WHAT'S NEXT?

"OK, Barnard Hill Park next stop," the male Animal Control officer said, more to himself than any of the animals in the transport cages, as he slid the van door closed.

"How do they know where to take us?" Pixie said from her cage with Chuck.

"That's how Oz identified us to the security guard, remember?" Frank the crow said from his cage with Simone. The van rattled along with no one saying anything for a moment.

Mo let out a big sigh. "Too bad we didn't tell them we were from someplace really nice like Jamaica."

This started a chorus of places the animals would have liked to have gone and complaints about Oswald and his "big mouth."

"Come on, you guys, simmer down," Tessa raised her voice to be heard. "You can't blame Oswald—you can't plan for things going wrong—"

There was a loud raccoon chortle. "Yeah, who has to *plan* for things to go wrong when you've got Oswald along?" Mo said. Some of the animals told him off for his comment; others were quiet.

Oswald shook his head. "It *was* my fault. I've ruined things again."

Queenie was in the same cage with Oswald and gave him a lick behind his ear. "Come on. None of us knew about those rules about needing a human along with us to get in the school."

The van came to a stop and the door slid open. The two Animal Control officers swung the cages out and walked them onto the green before opening them.

"OK, everyone. Last stop—all passengers must disembark!" The male officer chuckled. The female officer ticked off each animal from a list as they got out of the cages and sauntered off.

Oswald stopped by the man and looked up. "Excuse me, sir, who do we contact to schedule the assembly Principal Grant spoke of? You know—the one the *Washington Post* was going to cover?"

"What?" The man looked uncomfortable. "Um, I'm afraid that was a fib."

"The whole thing . . . a fib?"

"Um, we just needed to get you guys out of there."

"Hold on a second," the female Animal Control officer said. "This cat's someone's pet." She swooped Queenie up and tugged at her pink collar. "But there's no ID tag."

"I'm microchipped. And I live right here on Taylor Street. I can show you," Queenie said.

"I believe you, but we have to take you back to base, contact your owner, that sort of thing," the woman said and put Queenie back in the transport cage. "Sorry, cat," she said, and she sounded it. "Regulations."

"Oh, please let me out here. I'm *so* close." Her meows were heartbreaking. With a click and swoosh of the van door, she could no longer be heard.

I'm a complete failure. And *I'm doing harm to others . . . again.* Oswald wished he could disappear.

The rest of the animals stretched, scratched, and chatted.

"Did you see the look on her face when he—" Mo said.

Tiny guffawed and wiped a tear from his eye.

"Oh, I *know!* And then when the—" Reggie said. Frank flapped his wings as he laughed. Pixie did an imitation—of exactly who, Oswald wasn't sure. Even the shy Esmeralda was giggling as they all retold what happened.

I might as well miss the part when they start making fun of me. Oswald sighed, looked around for a bush, and started to crawl under it. *I know I would, if the pad was on the other paw.*

"Ow!" Oswald said. Someone had pulled his tail. He turned around and saw Frank hopping up and down, his shiny black eyes aimed at him.

"Come on, we're going to the garbage buffet. It's recycling tonight—lots of cans with stuff still in!" He turned and walked toward the others.

Oswald poked his nose out from under the bush and looked at all these wonderful animals.

"There you are!" Mo said and loped up to him. "What a day, eh?" He grinned. "You should see Pixie's imitation of Ms. Tinderclaw."

Oswald stepped out and sniffed the air. "If you're sure."

Hazel ran up and down a tree chattering, "Great time, great time, we had a great time!" She jumped off the tree and vaulted after Mo and the rest of the animals. Oswald waddled as fast as he could to catch up. Their laughter and storytelling pulled him closer. Tiny looked over his shoulder.

"Hey, Oz, hurry up!"

Oswald felt undeserving of their friendship and kindness. He was scurrying past boxes of recycling when something caught his eye; he stopped to look. There on the top page of a stack of newspapers was a photo of Joey and Naja, along with a story about some animal center.

24

NAJA ARRIVES

It was Thursday afternoon, and Joey watched the clock over the classroom door. He mostly liked school, but Naja was supposed to be at his house by this time. His mom arranged to work an early shift so she could be there when Ms. Harris brought her. The people from the animal refuge had come twice already to set up the pool and to mend the fence around their yard. This was to protect her from dogs and other animals.

Joey was surprised at how big the pool was—about twenty feet long and eight feet wide. It was shallow, one of those aboveground ones. They said it was important for her to be able to work her other muscles, given her wing injury. Ms. Harris would teach Joey and his mother how to help Naja exercise.

The bell rang. Joey sprang from his seat and out the door.

"Hi, Joey. Have you seen your animal friends again?" Valeria said as he rushed past her classroom.

"What? Oh, no. Oswald, the possum who did a lot of the talking? He used to live in my yard. But . . . well, it's a long story."

"Oh. Well, I'm coming with my mom on Sunday to your barbeque. Maybe I could meet him then?" Ria said.

Joey blinked and looked at her. He never paid much attention to her. Not because she wasn't nice. She was OK. But his mother seemed to think that just because she was friends with someone who had a kid close to his age, he and whoever that kid was should be friends. Of course, it didn't work like that. He knew his mother knew that, really, but she didn't always act like it.

"I didn't know you spoke Animal. You know, the day the animals came to the school, that was you who helped them find me, right?" he said.

Ria slung her purple-and-yellow knapsack over her shoulder. "Oh, yeah. We used to have a dog and I could always talk to her, but she got old and died. My mom says we can get another one this summer." A river of kids and teachers poured past them.

"Our neighbors have a dog, Zola. She'll be at the barbeque. You'll like her. She's great. But I've got to go. We have a goose coming to live with us today," Joey said.

"A goose? How'd you get a goose?"

Joey was moving down the hall. "I'll tell you Sunday."

Joey jogged down Thirty-Second Street, not stopping to say hello to the various pets as he usually did. He turned right on Perry Street and banged the gate open, then remembered to close it, now that Naja was here.

Ms. Harris, his mom, and Naja were in the yard by the pool. Mr. and Mrs. Edwards were there too, but not Zola. Melvin sat on the back deck watching the proceedings, tail swishing. Naja was walking around the yard, looking under bushes, waddling along the fence line, poking her beak at the bottom as though she was testing it. Her walk was awkward.

"Hi, Joey," Ms. Harris said and ruffled his hair. Joey hated when people did that, but tolerated it with Ms. Harris, not knowing her well enough to tell her.

"Hi, Ms. Harris. Hey, Mom, Mr. Edwards, Mrs. Edwards. What's Naja doing? Is she trying to get out?"

His mom gave him something between a hug and a wrestling hold around his shoulders. "No, don't worry. She's checking out her new territory. It's natural. She explained it all to me," his mother said.

"Ms. Harris explained it?" Joey said.

"No, Naja." His mother beamed. "I'm starting to understand her. Getting a little taste of your world."

25

A BUNCH OF HEADS ARE BETTER THAN ONE

Thursday afternoon in the park, Oswald lay spread-eagled on the hot grass. He was feeling very low after seeing that picture of Naja with Joey in the newspaper the day before. That was after Animal Control had brought them back to the park after their school visit.

"My life is here now, with all of you fine beings," Oswald told his fellow animals, as a means of trying to raise his own spirits. But when he looked up, he saw they had all moseyed on toward a road known for its excellent garbage buffet.

"Omigod, your face is longer than your tail!" Mo moaned, when Oswald caught up with them. Mo was sitting on the sidewalk, reaching up to his shoulder into a jar with a few pickles at the bottom.

"That's not helpful," Tessa said then climbed into a potato chip bag.

Pixie was munching on grass she brought to the dinner, not liking much else when it came to food. "I'm sorry, Oswald. I know what it's like to lose someone you love."

"But Joey's not lost—he's just a few blocks away. We can't give up yet!" Chuck exclaimed.

"Oh," Oswald said, but it sounded more like a sigh. His tail wrapped and unwrapped itself around his front leg. "I *knew* there was more to it when Joey said there was a lot going on at home. They don't want me and they don't need me anymore. Joey has Naja now—"

"Oh, for goodness' sake, can't a guy have more than one friend?" Mo huffed.

"Well, why don't we *do* something about it, besides yakking?" Tiny said.

"You think? You think it's worth trying again?" Oswald said.

They all shouted out ideas: Chuck suggested giving Joey a cardboard box he'd seen in the alley; Reggie offered his tinfoil collection; Pixie suggested she redecorate Miss Ann's house; and Hazel and Tessa volunteered to gnaw through anything that Joey might need disposing of. But, one by one, they realized the ideas were no good. It was late, and their ideas were only getting worse, so they agreed to all meet up again the next day and think some more.

But as they all started off toward their respective nests, the sound of a ringing bell made them stop. It was Queenie. She ran up to them with a big cat grin, ears perked forward, and eyes large and round.

"Hey, good to be back. I'll tell you that for free! My humans wouldn't let me out for a whole day—afraid I'd 'get lost' again." She plopped down among them and gave a good shake.

"And then they got the bright idea for this stupid bell." The animals shook their heads and made sympathetic noises.

"Queenie—lovely to see you. I am ever so sorry for any problems I may have inadvertently caused," Oswald said.

"Don't be silly. I loved going with you guys to Joey's school. That was the best adventure I've had for a long time. So, what did I miss? Any good parties?" Queenie asked.

And that gave Oswald exactly the idea they'd been looking for. But they only had two days to prepare.

26

OLD TRUSTY RUSTY

Friday afternoon after school, Joey sat on the Edwardses' porch. He watched the scene at his house. His mom sat on their front porch. Naja was in the blue laundry basket with one side cut away, for easier entrance and exit. Melvin sat on the table, sniffing Miss Ann's mug of herbal tea.

"You don't like my tea, remember?"

"I was hoping for coffee," Melvin said.

"Hmm, it's true. Cat's *do* like good service," his mom called over to Joey. She smiled. She was starting to understand Melvin now, too.

Joey laughed.

"No one said it was all good, what you'd hear when you understand Animals," Mrs. Edwards said. She poured lemonade into glasses.

"I hear that," Miss Ann said to Mrs. Edwards then turned to Naja. "You ready?" She got up, and the goose struggled out of the basket. A plastic tube was fitted over her broken wing. It still dragged, but she was able to move it a little.

Joey slurped the homemade lemonade. He whispered, "I don't know what to do for my mom's birthday. I don't have much allowance saved up—not enough to buy anything nice."

"Not so good at planning ahead?" Zola said. She got up and went inside.

"Don't you worry about that. Why don't we make her a birthday cake?" Mrs. Edwards said.

"Oh, Lordy," Mr. Edwards said, then got up with his newspaper and headed toward the door.

"What's wrong with that?" Mrs. Edwards said.

"Not a thing. I'll stay out of the way, is all. I know how you get when things don't go right between you and cake." He opened the screen door like he was about to go inside when Zola walked out with a blanket in her mouth.

"Don't listen to him, Joey. I'm a fine baker. Now what's her favorite?"

Joey thought a minute. "Lemon with raspberry stuff in the middle, I think."

"We can manage that. It'll be our little secret." Mrs. Edwards put her finger to her lips.

"Until the oven blows up." Mr. Edwards grinned.

"Oh, you stop it."

Zola put the blanket at Joey's feet. "This is my favorite. You could give it to your mom for her birthday."

Joey looked at Mrs. Edwards for guidance about how not to hurt Zola's feelings. Mrs. Edwards responded, "That is so sweet, Zola. But I *know* that's your favorite. How about you play 'Happy Birthday' on the keyboard for Miss Ann instead? I think that would be more special."

"You think?" Zola cocked her head to the side with her ears perked up.

Joey didn't know anything about Zola playing the keyboard and thought he must have misunderstood, but he didn't want to ask about it now.

"Absolutely. You are a dear, you know," Mrs. Edwards said to Zola, who nuzzled her big head under Mrs. Edwards's hand. "Joey, why don't you go help with Naja's training? Looks like you're missing all the fun." Mrs. Edwards nodded toward Joey's yard.

Naja and Melvin stood on the grass facing Miss Ann. Joey's mom led them in exercises; she lifted her arm, and the goose and cat lifted wing and paw—right, left, right, left.

"Thanks for making the cake and everything," Joey said in low tones to Mrs. Edwards.

"It'll be fun. Come along Sunday morning around nine thirty." Mrs. Edwards whispered.

Joey bounded back to his yard and stood next to his mom as Naja continued with her workout. Right wing up, left wing up—that was the hurt one.

"She needs to be up on something so she can move that wing better without bumping into the ground," Melvin said. He'd stopped doing the exercises and sat like a sphinx in the sun.

His mother turned to Joey, who interpreted as she still didn't understand everything the cat said.

"That makes sense . . . Let's see . . . " She looked around the yard.

"I know," Joey said and hurried toward the garage. "I'll get my old wagon."

Joey returned pulling his old, trusty, rusty red wagon. It rattled across the yard.

"Great idea," Naja said and waddled up to Joey. Miss Ann lifted Naja and placed her on the wagon, then led the way, walking around the yard, lifting one arm then the other, saying, "Right—up, two, three. Left—up, two . . . " Joey walked backward, pulling the wagon slowly.

"That's good, Naja. Keep going," Joey said.

Melvin watched from the deck. Naja held up both wings at once as Miss Ann counted.

Naja gave some happy honks. "Thank you. The air across my wings again is heaven." Joey sped up, and Naja lifted both wings at the same time again, momentarily lifting off above the wagon—she looked delighted. Then, like a rock in his stomach, the reality of helping Naja hit Joey. If this all went well, eventually Naja would leave them. He was happy for her, but his heart sank.

27

WAGON TRAIN

"That should do it," Mr. Edwards said. He stood back and smiled. Joey pushed his bike forward watching his trusty, rusty wagon roll along, hitched to the back.

"This is great, Mr. Edwards. Thanks," Joey said. He put the kickstand down and ran to the pool where Naja was paddling around on this hazy Saturday.

"It's ready, Naja. Let's give it a try," Joey said. The goose coasted to the edge, where there was a wooden ramp, and waddled out. She followed Joey, her left wing dragging less. Mr. Edwards and Joey lifted Naja on top of a couple of towels in the wagon. Naja nestled in, faced forward, then spread her wings, the plastic-tube splint still on the left one.

"Ready," she said.

Melvin opened his eyes to yellow slits. He had been sleeping on a chair on the back deck. Joey pedaled forward on the grass as Mr. Edwards walked next to Naja in the wagon.

"Go a little faster, let's make sure it holds," Mr. Edwards said. Joey obliged. Naja opened her wings about halfway. The air rippled her feathers. Naja opened and closed her wings a few times. Joey looked back and thought it looked like Naja was smiling, although he knew that wasn't possible.

"I think you're ready for the road," Mr. Edwards said.

"I'll go get my helmet." Joey parked his bike with Naja still in the wagon and bounced up the deck steps.

"What about me?" Melvin said. He stretched his body into a ski-slope shape. Joey stopped while holding the door to the house open.

"I want to go, too," the cat said.

"Sure, hop in. The front basket's all yours." Joey was inside getting his helmet when the doorbell rang. He could hear his mother say hi to Mrs. De Leon, Valeria's mom. He grabbed his helmet and went into the kitchen. Mrs. De Leon and his mom were maneuvering a large pot into the fridge.

"That's one big pot of veggie chili. Thanks, Lucia," Miss Ann said.

"Hi, Mrs. De Leon," Joey said.

She smiled. "Hi, Joey. I swear, you are taller and more handsome every time I see you," she said.

"Thanks, I guess. Is Ria here?" Joey said.

"Sorry, Joey. She wanted to come, but she had soccer practice. Do you want me to tell her anything? She's coming tomorrow."

Joey was surprised to feel a little disappointed. It would have been fun to show her his bike and wagon with Naja in it. "No, that's OK. I just wanted to show her the goose and stuff."

His mom gave Mrs. De Leon some sort of look. *Like kids don't notice this sort of thing.*

"I hear you're the Dr. Dolittle of Mount Rainier," Mrs. De Leon said.

"Yes, Joey has a lot of talent with animals," his mom said, drying her hands on a towel. "Let's go see how Naja's doing. Have to admit, it's been really neat helping her get better."

The three went out the door.

Melvin was waiting in the basket at the front. Mr. Edwards and Mrs. De Leon said hello, having met each other before.

"OK—let's get this party started," Melvin said.

Miss Ann and Mr. Edwards laughed.

"You guys know what he said?" Mrs. De Leon said.

Ann waved away the question. "Only sometimes, and believe me it's not always a blessing." Melvin shot her a look.

Joey walked the bike with the wagon and goose, basket and cat across the yard to the front gate with his mom, Mrs. De Leon, and Mr. Edwards behind. Joey pedaled off, increasing his speed. Naja flapped, rose up a few seconds, then settled down again. She did it again. Joey glanced over his shoulder and grinned—he *was* happy for her. It felt amazing to be part of this, helping Naja and seeing his mother become more of an animal person. Maybe his life was getting better. Out of the corner of his eye, he saw the three grown-ups, a proud triangle—his mother clasping her hands over her mouth, she looked like she might cry.

Joey pedaled on. He could feel Naja lifting off and landing, over and over. "You're doing it, Naja—you're flying!" Joey whooped and laughed. He turned up Thirty-Second Street and pressed up the hill.

"You go, goose-girl!" Melvin closed his eyes into the wind and held onto the basket.

"Hey, Joey. Wow—what have you got there?" A tall boy from the sixth grade called from the sidewalk. Joey stopped the bike, panting from the effort. Melvin spoke to the boy, but he didn't understand Animal.

"What did he say?" Ghalib, the sixth grader, said.

"He introduced himself and asked you your name. He's Melvin."

"Hi, I'm Ghalib," the boy said.

"This is Naja," Joey said. "That goose I was telling you about."

"That's really cool," Ghalib said. "Teaching a bird how to fly—"

Naja honked.

"What?"

"Fly *again*. She wants to make sure you realize she already knew how before the accident," Joey said.

Ghalib shook his head. "Wow, that's kind of weird and deep at the same time—you understanding animals like that."

Joey shrugged. "It's nothing. Hey, we're having a barbeque tomorrow. My mom's birthday. But it's no big deal. You want to come?" Joey said.

"I don't know. I *can* eat my share of barbeque. You sure you'll have enough?" Ghalib grinned.

"Oh, yeah. My moms always makes too much food. See you around one o'clock tomorrow, then," Joey said. He hoped he didn't look too desperate.

Ghalib shrugged. "OK, cool. Thanks. See you then."

Joey hightailed it back to his house. He almost forgot Naja was in the wagon. She spread her wings and lifted off for moments at a time.

His mom was on the phone when Joey burst in, letting the screen door slam.

"Joey—no door slamming!" she yelled out, then she said back into the phone, "Sorry about that. You have kids?" There was a pause and she laughed. "Yes, that's about right. OK, yes. We'll look forward to it. You and the photographer are welcome to stay for the barbeque—at least make yourself a plate." There was another pause. "Yes. It's all good. Great. See you then."

She hung up the phone and turned to her son. "Joey, the newspaper's coming tomorrow, probably during the barbeque. They want to do a follow-up story on Naja. One of those feel-good success stories about animals recovering. I'll need you to help me straighten up the house, OK?" She started picking things up and fluffing pillows.

"What? Oh, right—sure," Joey said, only half-listening, before spilling out what was on his mind. "Naja's getting a lot stronger. She lifted off a bunch of times. Then we saw Ghalib. He's in the sixth grade. He's real nice and everything. I invited him to the barbeque tomorrow. I know I'm supposed to ask you first, before I invite anybody to the house, and I'm really sorry, but would it be OK this one time if he came? If I promise to never do it again, and do all the dishes, and—"

"Whoa. Slow down. You invited a friend to the barbeque? That's great, Joey."

28

GOOD NEIGHBORS

On Sunday morning, the sky was covered with thick, puffy clouds like gray marshmallows. Joey arranged paper plates, napkins, and plastic knives, forks, and spoons on the dining room table. His mother chopped vegetables and made a fruit salad.

"Joey—come give me a hand, please." His mom was standing by the fridge, the door trying to close on her. "Hold this open, will you?"

"Sure, Mom." He held the door while she struggled with the large pot of vegetarian chili.

"I do not know who Lucia thinks is coming—a vegetarian army?" She lugged the pot to the stove.

"But it's really good," Joey said.

"Go ahead and put the drinks in the fridge, now that I've made room. I'm going to go upstairs for a catnap before everyone comes. Can you feed Naja and let her out into the yard?"

"Sure."

"You say anything besides 'sure'?"

"*Sure.*"

"That's my boy." She ruffled his hair. Joey ducked, grinned, grabbed the stacks of cups on the counter, and dashed out of the kitchen.

◆ ◆ ◆

Joey let himself into the Edwardses' house, closing the screen door softly behind him. It smelled like breakfast. Jazz played on the music system.

"Hey, Mrs. Edwards, Mr. Edwards," Joey called out.

Zola sat up from her spot on a blanket on the turquoise couch. She almost toppled the weird-looking lamp on the side table by wagging her tail. She had a big pink bow around her neck.

"There you are," Mrs. Edwards said as she entered the living room, wiping her hands on a towel. "Would you like pancakes and bacon, before we get started?"

"Thank you, but I already had breakfast," Joey said.

"Well, that doesn't have to stop you—you're a growing boy."

"OK, then—yes, please."

"Can I have some, too?" Zola said to Mrs. Edwards.

Mrs. Edwards had already started back to the kitchen. "Of course, you both get some." Boy and dog followed her.

"What's with that dumb bow, Zola?" Joey said.

Zola looked hurt. "You don't like it?"

Mrs. Edwards gave Joey a look. "Zola's dressed up for the party. Doesn't she look nice?"

"Oh. Right. Sorry, Zola. I don't know anything about girls' clothes." Sometimes he almost forgot Zola was a girl, what with her size and scruffy wiry fur. She had a number of scars and limped sometimes. Joey could tell she didn't want to talk about whatever it was that happened, so he never pressed it.

Joey wolfed down his pancakes with real maple syrup and crispy bacon—just how he liked it. Meanwhile, Mrs. Edwards measured ingredients into bowls, melted butter in the microwave, and got the mixer out.

Mr. Edwards appeared from the study next to the kitchen. "OK, Zola, all ready for your practice. Oh, hi, Joey. Here for your lesson in explosives and expletives?" Mr. Edwards said.

"Say what you like. Guess you won't want any of this lemon-raspberry cake with coconut icing?" Mrs. Edwards said as she retrieved two round cake pans.

"Oh, I'll get me a nice big slab, don't you worry. Does Joey have time to see Zola play before you two start?" Mr. Edwards said.

"Sure," Mrs. Edwards said.

Zola led the way into the study. There was a set of pedals from an electric organ on the floor, wired up to the keyboard. Mr. Edwards made a sweeping gesture toward the pedals. "And now I bring you the lovely Miss Zola on foot, or as we call them, paw pedals!" Mr. Edwards made the sound of a crowd cheering by blowing into his hands.

Zola nodded her head in a little bow. With her right front paw, she plunked out "Happy Birthday" without a single mistake. She turned and sat down facing Mr. Edwards and Joey.

"Wow!" Joey said.

"Do you think your mom will like it?" Zola said.

"Like it? She'll LOVE it!" Joey said and gave the dog a big hug. She thumped her tail hard against the wooden floor.

"Joey?" Mrs. Edwards called from the kitchen. "I need your help."

29

COMFORTS OF HOME

Slashes of blue cut through the clouds as Oswald waddled up to Joey's front gate, Mo beside him. Melvin was asleep on a chair on the porch.

"Say something." Mo elbowed Oswald.

"I will. I will," Oswald said.

Melvin opened one eye, then the other. He huffed when he saw Oswald, curled in the other direction, and draped his front paw over his eyes.

"Wait here," Oswald said to Mo, then squeezed under the gate and tiptoed up the steps.

"Melvin, may I speak with you for a moment?"

Melvin sighed, still facing away from him. "I guess."

"I've come to make amends. You have every right to be upset with me." Oswald's breath caught. "It is good to see you, Melvin." Oswald took a step back and sat down. Melvin turned his head and opened his eyes.

"Do you realize the damage you've done?" Melvin said. Oswald glanced over his shoulder at Mo waiting on the other side of the fence. Mo nodded in a way that said, "Take your time."

Oswald hung his head. "I know. And not just here either. But, I've come back to make it up to everyone. To Joey and Miss Ann in particular."

Melvin sat up and faced Oswald. "How do you plan to do that?"

"I've come with a few friends to make Miss Ann's birthday barbeque extra special. After all, what else is there besides spending time with friends, eh?" Oswald said.

Melvin looked over Oswald's head, saw Mo sitting on the grass next to the sidewalk, inspecting his claws and whistling. "Who's that?"

"That's Mo."

"Hi," Mo said and waved. "Nice to meet you—I've heard so many nice things about you. There's a few more of us waiting." He gestured down Perry Street toward Eastern Avenue. There was the sound of grass crunching and branches rustling as the animals took a few steps closer.

"Hmm. It would be nice to make this party special. There aren't a lot of folks to do things for Miss Ann. But we've got to think of Naja," Melvin said then paused. "You know. The goose who crashed into *your* newspaper after *you* made Joey read it to you that night? The goose who broke her wing?" Melvin said.

"I know . . . I know," Oswald said in a small voice.

"May I?" Mo pointed to the gate with his nose.

"It's a free country," Melvin said and jumped off the chair.

Mo ambled up the steps and sat about five feet away from Melvin. "We've gotten to know Oz here pretty well," Mo said.

"I'm all ears," Melvin said.

"And I know he used to come across a bit, um, single-minded," Mo said.

"If you mean having his mind singularly on himself," Melvin said, twitching his tail.

Oswald let out a splutter. He looked away.

Mo chuckled, glanced at Oswald. "He really has changed, or maybe these good parts were always in him."

Melvin cocked his head. Oswald started stepping from paw to paw to paw to paw.

"Please, Melvin. Let us do this. We've been working on it for days—well, two, anyway." He gestured toward the others.

Melvin wove through the chair legs and gave Oswald a sniff. "Well, OK. After all, Miss Ann saved me. I would have been put down if she hadn't adopted me from the animal shelter. Let me know what I can do to make her birthday one to remember."

Oswald made a chattering noise, and the animals emerged from shrubs and trees. Tiny and Chuck, the rats Reggie and Tessa, Hazel, Esmeralda the opossum, and Frank the crow made their way into the yard. They carried and dragged things. The rats and Hazel screeched to a stop when they saw Melvin on the porch.

Reggie stood on his hind legs, with one short forelimb across Tessa and the other across Hazel. "You didn't say anything about a cat."

"Of course we did. Remember—that's why Queenie decided not to come," Tiny said.

"Nope. Don't remember that," Reggie said, with his arms still protecting Tessa and the squirrel. "Must have been when I went to get pizza crusts for everyone."

"Don't worry your pointy little faces," Melvin said. "I'm not a mouser, OK?"

"My face isn't pointy," Hazel said.

"All right if we get started?" Tiny asked.

"Of course. By the way, that's Naja over there swimming around in the pool. I'll let you introduce yourselves," Melvin said then went into the house.

The animals followed him in and got to work. Frank draped streamers around the lights on the ceilings. Tiny blew up balloons with a pump then handed them to Mo, who tied them.

It was Chuck's job to stick the balloons up with pieces of tape Frank tore off.

Esmeralda got bunches of wildflowers and weeds out of a plastic bag and set out to find some vases. There was a tapping at the door.

"Oh, right. Forgot to mention. A few more are coming," Oswald said.

"*More*?" Melvin said.

Oswald nosed the screen door open. "It's Pixie and Simone," he called over his shoulder toward Melvin. "The band should arrive in a little while."

"A band? Pixie and who?" Melvin said.

Simone and Pixie walked in, dragging a plastic bag between them. Pixie stepped toward Melvin. She was wearing what looked like a brightly colored beaded lampshade. The beads jingled as she extended her right front paw toward Melvin. "Hi, you must be Melvin. I'm Pixie. Nice to meet you."

Melvin looked unsure, "Um, nice to meet you." Then he whispered to Oswald, "Why is she wearing a, um, a *dress*?"

Tiny had sidled up to them. He whispered, "She thinks she can pass as human." Then, to the skunk and groundhog, "Hey, you guys made it! What have you got there?" he guided them into the house.

Simone pulled the plastic bag with her teeth, backing further into the house. Pixie smiled her toothy grin. "It's a present for Miss Ann—a dress. It's something we've upcycled. I hope she likes it. We had to guess her size . . . " Her words faded into the hum of activity as she followed Simone.

Melvin looked around at the hubbub. "We've got to keep it down. Miss Ann's gone upstairs for a nap before the party."

"I'll go tell them," Oz said. "And where's Joey?" He felt a pang of warmth and longing at saying his name.

"He's next door, making a cake with Mrs. Edwards. It's a surprise," Melvin said.

"Got it," Oswald said then scampered off to oversee the party preparations. Streamers were going up, chairs were being pushed to different places, Reggie was arranging a load of pizza crusts he'd collected just for the party, and Chuck and Mo were on the couch plumping pillows.

"That's OK, guys, I think the pillows are fine," Oz said.

"Just wanted to check," Chuck said.

"Hey, I've always wanted to sit on a couch—I can see why they're so popular," Tiny said as he spread himself out and closed his eyes.

Oswald was relieved when he heard faint mariachi music from outside; relieved because they came, and because this could keep the raccoons busy and off the furniture. "Tiny, Chuck, the band's here. We need your help." The raccoons jumped off the sofa and joined Oswald at the door.

Eight raccoons, in long skirts, puffy white blouses, and large-brimmed straw hats filed up the porch. They each carried an instrument case and introduced themselves by number. One through Eight filed through the door and inside the house.

"Excuse me, who's Melvin? I understand he's the sound cat," Number Five said.

"I'm your cat," Melvin called out as he walked up to them.

Pixie rushed up to Oswald. The glass beads on the lampshade clinked. "We've arranged the dress on a chair in the study. I think she'll really be surprised. What else can I do?"

Oswald opened and closed his mouth a few times. Pixie was desperate to be helpful ever since the unfortunate mistaken identity incident.

Tiny hurried up to them and gave Oswald a look. He put a paw around Pixie, and aimed her toward the back door. "I have an important job for you, if you wouldn't mind."

"Of course not, I'm here to serve!" Pixie's eyes shone. Tiny escorted her out to the back deck.

Esmeralda crept out from under the couch and up to Oswald. "How do you do it? How do you keep from fainting with all this commotion?"

Oswald started to answer her, but Frank yanked him away with questions about streamers, and then Tessa asked Oswald to sort out an issue with the balloons.

Feeling apprehensive about the brouhaha of the party, Esmeralda slunk from room to room, and then into the kitchen. Finally, her natural urge to go up when scared got the better of her. She climbed onto a chair, and then onto the kitchen counter.

"Ooh, looks like one of those mud baths Oswald talks about. She slid the top off the large pot of chili and tested it with her snout. "Mmm, perfect temperature, too. Don't mind if I do," she said, climbing in.

30

YOU NEVER KNOW WHAT'S COOKING IN SOMEONE ELSE'S POT

"Miss Ann's getting ready to come downstairs!" Tessa said as she skittered to the rest of the animals.

"Everyone, keep it down," Oswald whispered. He stood on the dining room table, the animals gathered below and around him. His tail automatically wrapped and unwrapped itself around his front leg. "In that case, we won't do a sound check," Oswald said. Tiny nodded his approval. The Mariachi band stood at the ready with their instruments.

Although he wouldn't admit it to Esmeralda, Oswald was also struggling not to faint with all the chaos, never mind his new role as leader. He appreciated Tiny's and Melvin's help. Everyone waited in silence.

The back door slammed open and Oswald winced. "Shh, everyone!" he whisper-shouted. They could hear Pixie humming to herself and her lampshade bumping against things. Oswald looked at Tiny, who hurried out of the room. The clock on the wall ticked. Tiny rushed back in. "I got her to stay out of the way—in the kitchen," he whispered.

They could hear things being moved around and the clang of a pot lid. Tiny started to go back in, but Oswald indicated for him to stay as he heard Miss Ann's footsteps coming down the stairs.

Oswald spied Joey through the window, on the Edwardses' porch, carrying the cake. He'd be here any second. It took all of Oswald's strength to not forget everything he was doing and run out and throw his paws around him.

Miss Ann's footsteps grew nearer.

"Now!" Oswald whispered.

The band struck up a boisterous rendition of "Las Mañanitas."

The doorbell rang. *Why would Joey ring the doorbell?*

There was a soft groaning coming from the kitchen. *Why can't that groundhog keep quiet for a few minutes?*

Miss Ann rushed in. "What in the world is going on?"

"Happy Birthday!" the animals yelled.

A man with a woman was tapping on the screen door. "Sorry we're early. Ms. Jones?" Joey stood on the porch behind these two people, holding the cake.

"No problem. Please, come in. Looks like everything's started early."

The moans and groans got louder.

The band got louder, still playing the classic Mexican happy birthday song.

"Joey? What's going on here?" Ann yelled over the music as she rushed through the house, stepping past animals, over balloons, and brushing streamers out of her way.

The reporter and photographer followed her. The band played on at top volume.

Strange squeaks and chirps came from the kitchen. "Joey!? What on earth is going on?" Ann dashed into the kitchen, the reporters at her heels.

The chili was spilling over. The lid on the pot moved up and down—an odd sound grew louder each time the lid went up. Ann flung the lid off. She gasped and plunged her hand into the warm chili. She pulled out a limp opossum.

Ann immediately started washing the chili off of Esmeralda. Joey stood at his mother's side, eyes big, still holding the cake.

Ann shook her head while she tried to rouse the possum. Ann did not look happy. "Is this some sort of joke, Joey? Is she playing dead?"

"Some sort of joke, indeed," the woman reporter said.

Ann shook her head. "I had no idea."

The photographer snapped pictures.

"I bet you didn't," the woman reporter said. She walked out of the room punching numbers on her phone.

Mr. Edwards leaned into the open window of a car. "The barbecue's off. It's a real shame."

"This must be some sort of mix-up, is all. Our Miss Ann would never do anything like that," the woman in the car said. They drove off.

There was an Animal Control van and a police car parked in front of the house.

An Animal Control officer and a police officer worked together, taking statements. The Animal Control officer did the talking to the animals. She crouched down and asked the Mariachi band, "Did any of you see how the opossum got in the pot of chili?"

"No. We were in the other room waiting to play, or playing," Number Three, the violinist, said.

"Is she dead?" the raccoon holding a *guitarrón* said.

"No, she just fainted," the Animal Control officer said. "The chili was only warm. But we'll have to take her in for a full exam—protocol."

"What did they say?" the police officer asked. The Animal Control officer got him up to speed.

The police officer took a business card out of his pocket. "Can you ask them to contact us if they remember anything else? We'll get an interpreter." The Animal Control officer gave the card to the raccoon with the fanciest dress. She joined her bandmates, and they headed out of Ann's yard through the front gate.

Another Animal Control officer walked up to the other officer.

"The goose didn't know anything. Was outside the whole time. She's cleared to go back to the animal refuge now. The cat, crow, and squirrel didn't see anyone put the possum in the pot," he said.

"Weird. No one I talked to saw anything either—not the band, not the three raccoons over there, and not the other possum," the first Animal Control officer said.

"Think they're covering for the human, this Ann Jones?" the police officer said.

"I don't know. Find anyone else?" the first Animal Control officer said.

"Nope. Not a soul. Just this," he said and held up the garish beaded lampshade.

◆ ◆ ◆

Joey sat on the front porch steps wiping his face with his sleeve. Oswald sat next to him. There was a cake with coconut icing on the table. Mr. Edwards walked up to them.

"You all right, son?" Mr. Edwards said.

"I was *so* scared. I thought it was Oswald." Joey heaved a breath. "What's going to happen now?"

Mr. Edwards leaned down and put his hand on Joey's shoulder. It looks like they're going to arrest your mom—put her in jail. Animal cruelty's a big deal—a real crime."

"But she didn't do it! And they said the possum's fine—just fainted! My mom would never do anything like that," Joey said.

Mr. Edwards straightened up. "I know she didn't do it—not our Miss Ann. But it doesn't look good—she was the only one, well, the only human in the house. The photographer got lots of photos—"

"But didn't the animals tell them she didn't do it?" Joey said.

Mr. Edwards let out more air than Joey thought his old lungs could hold. "I gather the animals didn't see anything. Didn't see how it happened."

Joey felt worried, scared, and guilty. If he wasn't such an animal person, if he hadn't been friends with Oswald, none of this would have happened. He thought for a minute.

"But why would she save that possum if she did it?" Joey worked hard to not cry.

The front screen door gave its friendly squeak, and Mrs. Edwards came outside, joining them on the porch. "Oh, Joey, I don't know. They think she did that because she was caught. And . . . "

"And what?" Joey said.

"They have her recorded on a phone call a while back. Remember when she called to have Oswald relocated that morning before you went to school? They recorded her saying she'd cook that possum next time she saw it," Mrs. Edwards said.

Joey burst into tears. Oswald padded on his paws back and forth, looking up at Joey. Mrs. Edwards brought Joey into a tight hug. He sobbed.

Ann came out of the house. She looked like she'd been crying, too. She reached for Joey and hugged him.

"This will all get sorted out. I promise. But now I need you to be my little man," his mother said. "OK?"

Joey nodded, "Always."

"Your dad's coming. You'll be staying with them for a while. Suzette will bring you back here to school. Mr. and Mrs. Edwards have kindly offered to look after Melvin. I'm afraid Naja will have to go back to the wildlife refuge."

"But her flying lessons. Mr. Edwards hitched my wagon up to my bike and everything . . . " Joey trailed off.

Miss Ann tipped Joey's face up toward hers. "I know. You've done wonderful things with Naja. Your dad said they'll try to take you to the animal center. You'll still get to see her."

Joey shrugged. He couldn't believe this was all really happening.

31

ICE CREAM

Joey twirled on the chair at the computer desk in the family room at his dad's house. He was trying to Skype Melvin, but there was no answer. He spun around again, turning the room into a kaleidoscope of brown sofa, red recliner chairs, and speckled carpet. A set of blocks half-built into something sat in the corner. A plastic purple horse with a pink mane was stuck in the crack of the couch. Noah and Mary were already in bed. Seeing his stepbrother's and stepsister's toys strewn about made him feel funny—like he didn't belong, but wanted to. He always felt normal with his dad. It was just Suzette and the kids he still felt a little uncomfortable around—like he had only just met them, each time. And it wasn't like Suzette didn't try. Sometimes she tried too hard, and that was just as bad.

The big TV on the wall was on low. The Wizards were playing the Detroit Pistons, an away game. Usually Joey would have been glued to the set, but not tonight.

Joey turned back to the computer screen and Skyped again, desperate for some connection to home. He couldn't even think about his mom in jail. He remembered hearing grown-ups sometimes say that "things were too awful to think about" and it never made sense, until now. Every time his brain got anywhere close to it, he felt like he might throw up. So he tried to keep his brain away from the topic.

He heard his name from the kitchen, so he clicked on the keyboard, pretending he was doing something on the computer. His dad and Suzette were finishing the dishes from supper, takeout Chinese they got because Joey liked it, but he couldn't eat much.

"You know, Joey can stay as long as he and Ann want. That was one of the reasons we bought this house, so he could have his own room," Suzette said.

Yup, trying too hard.

"I'll drive him to school. It's on my way to work anyway. I want to have a word with the principal if he has time. You're OK with picking him up?" Carlton said.

"Of course, no problem. Maybe he'll get more comfortable with me."

Don't count on it.

"Don't be silly. He's fine with you," Carlton said.

"Mm-hmm," Suzette said in that way that really meant, "Don't be stupid, we both know better."

Joey was shocked. He had no idea Suzette realized he didn't like her much. It wasn't that he didn't *like* her. She was nice enough. But Joey couldn't help but think that if it wasn't for her, his mom and dad would still be together. His mom told him that it wasn't like that. But he didn't believe her.

Skype jangled on the computer.

"Melvin, hi," Joey said.

"Hey, Joey. You OK? We're all worried about you," Melvin said.

"What do you mean 'we'? Who's there? Move. I want to see." A rat scurried across the desk right in front of Melvin.

"What was that?"

"That was Reggie—Reginald. He's cool. You'll like him."

"Is Oswald there?" Joey said.

"Yeah, he's staying here. Keeping everyone in line."

"*Everyone?* Melvin. The house *cannot* be messed up when my mom gets back."

"Don't worry. We'll keep it straight." Someone asked Melvin something off-camera. "I got to go. I'll catch you tomorrow. Love and peace, my human brother."

"Yeah, love, peace, out," Joey said.

Joey jumped with surprise when Suzette put her hand on his back. "Glad you're keeping in touch with your friends, furry or otherwise," she said. "Your dad will take you to school tomorrow, then I'll pick you up. I can take you to the animal refuge if you'd like. Your mom told me how good you are with that duck with the broken wing—"

"She's a goose," Joey said, surprised at the edge in his voice.

"I'm sorry, baby. I didn't mean to call your goose friend a duck," Suzette said.

Carlton snickered in the kitchen.

"No, I mean it—I understand how Joey feels. It would be like someone calling Mary or Noah lizards. Right?"

Carlton joined them in the family room, plopped down on the sofa, and grabbed the remote. "Or aliens. That'd be about right," Carlton said and chuckled.

"Noah—he's definitely an alien," Joey said. He gave his dad a high five.

"You two," Suzette said. "Who wants ice cream?"

32

THE LAST STRAW

After Miss Ann, Joey, and all the officers had left, the animals came out from under bushes and cars, or down from trees. Simone decided to go home, she was used to a quieter life. Melvin, Oswald, the rats, and Hazel the squirrel could all go into the house through the cat flap. But the raccoons were too big. And no one had seen Pixie since before they yelled *surprise*. Melvin stood on Oswald's back and opened the door from the inside. Luckily it was a lever-style handle. The raccoons came in.

"I owe everyone an apology," Oswald started. "Another one of my endeavors turned into a disaster." He shuddered. His tail made an attempt at wrapping around his forelimb and even it seemed to give up, flopping onto the floor next to him.

"Oh, for goodness' sake," Mo said, shaking his head. He walked up to the fridge and reached for the handle. "Get over yourself."

"Mo!" Tessa said.

Tiny joined Mo and peered into the now-open fridge. "Bless Mrs. Edwards—she put the leftovers in here. But Oz, Mo does have a point. Not everything is your fault." He pushed a plastic container onto the floor, then pushed it toward the living room.

"Hey—where's Pixie?" Chuck asked, interrupting his own foraging in the still-open fridge. He stood on his hind legs and grabbed slices of cheese off a plate.

Hazel found a bag of honey-roasted nuts in the cabinet and jumped down. "Are we eating in the living room?"

Tiny called over his shoulder, "Yeah, thought we'd watch TV."

Reggie and Tessa scampered toward the living room dragging carrot and celery sticks. "Pixie probably had something to do with Esmeralda getting into that pot of chili, don't you think?" Reggie said as he moved vegetables.

Frank cocked his head from his perch on top of the kitchen cabinets. "It is strange her being the only one missing. I have to admit." He hopped down next to Oswald.

The rest of them were in the living room now, except for Oswald and Frank. "Oh dear, this won't do," Oswald said aloud. He waddled over to the fridge to shut the door.

"Hold on a minute, I see some homemade mac and cheese, if you don't mind," Frank said.

"What? No, of course. Be my . . . Ann's guest. I guess," Oswald said. But Frank was already plodding backward, dragging the container across the floor toward the living room.

Oswald was listening to them talking about what to watch in the living room when he was distracted by the mess around him.

The fridge door, cabinets, and drawers were open. Food, utensils, unfurled paper towels, unrolled tin foil, and other odds and ends were strewn across the counters and floor. Melvin sauntered back in and over to his bowls. He took a long drink of water.

"Oh, Melvin." Oswald sat down on the floor with his head in his paws. "What a mess." Melvin lapped his water for another moment before turning around.

"Yup. Glad *I* didn't invite all these idiots over," Melvin said.

Oswald exhaled a possum-full of defeat. Melvin looked at him and twitched his tail.

"Hey, sorry man. That was harsh. What about I help clean up tomorrow? I'm supposed to stay at the Edwardses'. I better be going," Melvin said.

"Sure," was all Oswald could manage.

In the living room, all the animals were on the floor, except for the raccoons who certainly seemed fond of the couch. Tiny was holding the remote down while Frank pecked at the keys.

Chuck looked up at Oswald, "They've got Internet TV! Anything you want to watch?"

Oswald, deflated and heartbroken, didn't answer. They all sounded far away. He barely heard the sitcom laughter from the TV, along with their chatting, munching, and slurping. Reggie went in and out of the kitchen collecting things—a bottle cap, a button, a plastic straw.

Oswald heard scurrying upstairs. *Was someone* under *the floorboards?*

"Everyone, we need to talk," Oswald said.

"Shh. I want to see this," Mo said.

"NOW," Oswald said.

Frank turned the volume up.

"Can it wait 'til this is over? I love this show!" Tessa said.

Oswald walked out of the living room and into the study. *How can they be so thoughtless? And me, how could I have been so stupid to think this plan would ever work? Now I've more than done it. I've really ruined everything—and maybe for good.* Another episode of the comedy had started. His animal friends

laughed, chattered, and cawed at the show. The light of the television flickered into the study. Here he was, on the inside, but he still felt like he was on the outside. He went out the cat flap and trundled down the steps to his home under the deck and into his own bed.

33

THE SIT OF YOUR LIFE

Monday morning, a new day, a new week, Oswald told himself. He thought about going next door to the Edwardses' to see Zola and Melvin. *Maybe I should move out, too.* He smoothed his face while looking in his can-lid mirror. He saw a coward and a failure. He'd lost his best human friend, put the boy's mother in jail, and another possum was traumatized, all on his watch.

I need to get them out of the house.

He got out of his home from under the deck and stopped in his tracks when he heard her voice. Pixie. She was on the deck, braiding Tiny's tail as it hung through the back of a plastic chair. She was wearing a bright-orange plastic shopping bag, with holes for her head and arms. Her fur was decorated with twist ties, rubber bands, and a few pop-tops. She had her sparkly cat-eye glasses on and was chatting away.

"Now don't forget to tell everyone where you got your fur done," she said.

"I won't," Tiny said.

"Where have you been, Pixie?" Oswald said.

Pixie stopped braiding. "I heard the news. Terrible. Poor thing. Will she be all right?" Pixie gnashed her teeth.

"Yes, they think Esmeralda just fainted, more from all the pandemonium than anything else. The chili was only warm.

But they took her in for a full checkup, to be sure," Oswald said, "Where'd you go?"

Pixie started on another braid. "My sister's. I forgot she asked me to stop over."

"Oh," he said and started to go in when he saw that the cat flap had been removed and all that was left was a large hole.

He turned to Tiny, "How did this happen?"

Tiny craned his neck while Pixie continued her furdressing. "Oh, that. We enlarged it—removed the cat flap part so we larger beings can get in and out."

Pixie nodded confirmation.

Oswald started to protest, but lost strength and went into the house to see everything he was facing before choosing his battles.

The house was even more of a mess than yesterday. There were open takeout containers with food still in them. An empty pizza box on the dining room floor. Oswald heard voices, one unfamiliar. He peered into the living room. A huge raccoon with a bald tail and a patch over one eye, like a pirate, lolled on the couch.

"Oh, this is *good*. This is *real good*," Baldy said. Mo stood next to the couch like an usher at a theater. "Can I have another ten minutes? I've got the money," Baldy said as he wriggled back and forth, eyes closed.

"You'll have to get back in line. It wouldn't be fair to the others. But you can buy refreshments while you wait," Mo said.

The raccoon rolled off and wandered out the front door. A skunk came in and handed Mo some coins. After he studied them and clicked them against his teeth, he dropped them into a mug on the floor. He looked at a clock on the wall, "Your time starts . . . now," he said to the skunk who clambered up onto the couch.

Oswald went out the front door. There was a line of about ten animals on the porch and down the steps. These included raccoons, skunks, a porcupine, someone's dog—she had a collar—and a tortoise. Chuck had set up shop. There was food in piles, a tube of toothpaste, a bottle of ketchup, and juice boxes lined up under one of the old chairs.

"Two cents a squirt, ketchup or toothpaste," Chuck said to a skunk.

"How about one cent for the ketchup?" the skunk said.

"Can't do that, I'm afraid. This is premium brand stuff, my friend," Chuck said. He drummed his fingers on his stomach.

Oswald scurried down the steps and around the side of the porch before he hoisted himself up. "Psst. Chuck—what are you doing?"

Chuck startled, then broke into a grin. "Isn't this great? Where've you been? We've already made a dollar and thirty-five cents. We're going to split it fifty-fifty with Miss Ann to help with her legal fees."

"You can't sell time on the couch. What if someone goes to the bathroom on it?"

This got a roar of indignation from the waiting crowd.

"What sort of animals do you think we are?" huffed the tortoise.

"I'm house trained," the dog said. "I'm just not allowed on the furniture—"

"Oh, and a *couch*...," one of the waiting raccoons said, and almost swooned with the thought.

Oswald climbed onto the porch. This was not a private conversation anymore. Then he saw the sign taped to a porch post. In poorly drawn block letters it read:

THE SIT OF YOUR LIFE

TEN MINUTES ON A REAL COUCH

10 CENTS.

34

RIDE, NAJA, RIDE

Suzette waited in the minivan in front of Mount Rainier Elementary School. Joey was talking to Ghalib and Ria. After a few minutes, Suzette beeped the horn. He talked to his friends a little longer, then hopped in the car. Noah and Mary were strapped into their car seats in the back.

"In the back, Joey. Please," Suzette said. She seemed tense or annoyed. Joey smiled to himself, feeling bad—but not *that* bad—for irritating her. He got into the back seat and strapped in. He forgot she was one of those grown-ups who didn't let kids sit in the front. She drove off.

"Everything OK? Any news about my mom?" Joey said.

Suzette leaned forward, clutched the wheel, and made a turn.

"What? No. Joey, could you please get in the car when you see me and not make me wait?"

"Oh, right. Sorry. I was just saying good-bye to my friends."

"Hi, Joey," Mary said. "I made you a picture." She held up a crayon drawing of a beige and brown cat. "My mom says you have a cat like this."

"Thanks, Mary," Joey said.

"Hi, Joey-Joey," Noah said and beamed.

Joey chatted with Mary and Noah. The ride seemed longer than he remembered.

"Ducks!" Noah said, pointing out the window. It was the Merkle Wildlife Sanctuary sign with geese.

"Those are *geese*, Noah," Suzette broke her silence and caught Joey's eye in the rearview mirror.

"Hey, you brought me here!" Joey said.

"As promised. Ms. Harris said to go to her office. Are you all right going in on your own?" Suzette said as she stopped the car in front.

Joey was already halfway out. "Yeah, no problem."

"Great. Have fun. Your dad will pick you up," Suzette said and drove away.

Joey followed Ms. Harris into a large storage shed. There was wood lined up along the wall, fencing, fifty-pound bags of animal feed, other supplies, and equipment.

"Come take a look at these. See what you think," Ms. Harris said. Joey followed her around the large stacks of feed to three brightly colored, adult-sized tricycles. They looked more like bicycles in the front, with a two-wheeled carriage at the back. The carriage had a soft roof that looked like it folded down. Under this roof was a bench seat covered in red vinyl. That faced a smaller wooden bench, painted blue.

"Rickshaws," Ms. Harris said.

"What are they for?" Joey said.

"They *were* for giving rides to visitors, but it didn't catch on like we were hoping. After seeing the picture your mom posted of you training Naja with your wagon hitched to your bike—"

"My mom posted a picture of us?"

"Yes, on our Facebook page. That's how the newspaper got wind of it and arranged with your mom to go to the house again yesterday." Ms. Harris freed one of the rickshaws from the things around it and wheeled it to Joey. "Want to give it a try?"

"Sure."

Joey took the rickshaw from Ms. Harris. It was weird and cool at the same time.

"Naja's psyched you're coming. Her splint is off now, too.

Ms. Harris and Joey placed a piece of plywood across the two back seats. After a struggle, they folded down the roof. Joey pedaled the rickshaw, standing up to get going, and Ms. Harris walked alongside. Joey parked it in front of the flock disorder unit and ran in ahead of Ms. Harris.

Joey barely glanced over his shoulder to Ms. Harris. "That's OK—you go right ahead."

He flung the gate to Naja's pen open and hugged the goose, his head buried in her feathers.

"Gentle now," Ms. Harris said.

Joey was glad she hadn't asked a question, because the tears he'd been holding back since yesterday came out, all over Naja. She draped her long neck over his shoulder, and if he wasn't imagining it, she rubbed his back with her beak. This made him laugh, and he stood up.

"It's great to see you, Naja. Ready?" he said.

"It's good to see you too, Joey. Yes, let's go!" Naja said and gave her wings a gentle flap.

Ms. Harris held the door to the unit open for the boy and goose. "OK, you two." Joey and Ms. Harris lifted Naja onto the bench.

And off they went for the rest of the afternoon. Joey pedaled in long straightaways, checking on Naja over his shoulder. She would flap hard a few times, and Joey would speed up. Then she'd catch the air and glide, as Joey kept pedaling before she'd settle on the bench again. Joey counted her flaps aloud each time before takeoff—one, two, three, four, five, six—with Naja honking the count. Boy and goose, speeding and gliding, speeding and gliding. The wind in his face the same that lifted her wings.

35

BEAUTY FOR THE BEASTS

Zola sat on a chair on the Edwardses' porch. Oswald and Melvin were on the table. They watched the goings-on over at Miss Ann's this Tuesday morning. The line for "The Sit of Your Life" trailed off the porch, down the steps, and all the way to the front gate. A wire-haired dachshund walked into the yard.

"Excuse me. I'm looking for Beauty for the Beasts?" Ms. Dachshund said.

"In the back," came the chorus from the waiting couch sitters.

"See what I mean? The situation is out of control," Oswald said to Melvin and Zola.

Melvin grabbed his back leg like it might be trying to get away from him and washed it with gusto. "At least they're earning money toward Miss Ann's defense," Melvin said.

Oswald spluttered. "For goodness' sake. What could they have earned so far—ten, maybe twenty dollars? You can't get more than a few minutes with a lawyer for that."

"Yeah, but it's more than any of us are doing."

Oswald felt a hot flush run through him. He opened and closed his mouth, but said nothing. He took a few deep breaths before he could speak. "You have no idea how bad I feel," Oswald started to say. "How do I get rid of them?"

"I couldn't tell you. I haven't had my late-mid-morning nap yet," Melvin said and closed his eyes. "Oh, right—I promised to help with the mess. I will help, but later."

Zola shrugged. "I'll help later, too. But I'm about to go do some therapy right now. Mrs. Edwards is taking me in a few minutes."

Zola's a therapist? Oswald was surprised at how much he didn't know about his friends. He saw her in a new light—the scars, the stiff gait. Maybe this was all related. He was ashamed he'd never asked her more about her life before.

"Zola, that is very noble of you—being a therapy dog. I would love to hear all about it. Later, once I get all this back under control," Oswald said.

Zola looked at him as though she hadn't seen him properly before either. She cocked her head and blinked, "Sure . . . if you're interested."

Zola and Melvin exchanged looks.

"You feeling all right, man?" Melvin said to Oswald.

"Never felt better, my good friend. It's time I stepped up to the plate," Oswald said, took a deep breath, then marched down the steps from the Edwardses' porch.

He stomped up the steps to Ann's porch as loud as he could. "Excuse me, I have an announcement."

But no one paid him any mind. They continued their conversations and buying and eating snacks.

"I said *excuse me!*"

Still no one seemed to notice him.

"THE COUCH IS CLOSED UNTIL FURTHER NOTICE!"

Everyone stopped what they were doing and stared at him.

"But, Oswald, we're running a business. I thought you approved," Chuck said.

"I never said I approved. And now, I'm shutting it down!" Oswald said.

The screen door swung open. Mo came out, looked surprised. "What's going on, Oz? We have a good thing going here. It'll pay for more takeout."

"No, this has all gone too far. It's my fault, my responsibility, so I'm fixing it. Starting with you, couch sitters—out!" Oswald was surprised at the forcefulness in his voice.

A few animals sloped off. Others stood their ground.

"I already paid," a huge longhaired cat said. "I'm never allowed on the furniture; this is my only chance."

"Mo, give the gentleman his money back," Oswald said.

"Come on, Oz, it's only ten minutes," Mo said.

Oswald got into Mo's face, his triangular head eye to eye with Mo's masked one. "You know I have fifty sharp teeth . . . " Oswald paused and bared them without moving an inch. "And I will rearrange your stripes into an unflattering plaid if you don't give the cat his money back. Right now."

Mo stepped back and blinked. "OK, OK, no need to get your tail in a knot. I'll go get the cat his money." Mo went into the house.

"And will you critters stop telling me what to do with my tail!" Losing his temper was also new to Oswald. He climbed up onto the railing and ripped down the sign.

Mo came back out and counted out ten cents into a small pouch sewn onto the cat's collar. Tiny ambled out of the house.

"What's going on, Oz?" Tiny said.

Frank flew over and perched on the railing. "Everything OK?"

"Don't anyone move," Oswald said. The couch customers had all cleared off, leaving Oz, the raccoons, and Frank.

"Oz, what's wrong?" Tiny said in one of those ultra-calm voices folks save for crazy or violent beings.

"Why are you talking to me like that?" Oz said. "Like you're afraid of me. Or you're planning something."

"Whoa there, buddy. We *are* afraid of you. Aren't we, guys?" Tiny said. Frank, Mo, and Chuck nodded.

Oswald looked into their eyes—he didn't recognize his reflection. And he definitely didn't like it. He slumped on the porch and held his head in his paws. "I need your help."

No one said anything for a moment.

A delivery truck pulled up in front of the house. The delivery woman walked up to the door with a package. She nodded hello to the animals. "Says on here I can leave this on the front porch. Have a nice day." She put the package next to the door and left.

Oswald was surprised how loud rat paws could be. Tessa and Reggie skittered to a stop as they came out the front door. "I heard the truck. Must be that wonderful new lavender-scented quilt I bought," Tessa said.

"How on earth did you buy that?" Oz said.

"We found a credit card in the table next to Miss Ann's bed," Reggie said. "It works great. All you have to do is give the magic numbers and everyone gives you stuff. Takeout, buttons for my collection—"

Oz let out a long, harsh sound and covered his eyes. No one else moved a muscle. When he looked up, he said, "This . . . has . . . all . . . got TO STOP!"

The animals looked stunned.

Tiny stepped forward and kicked at a food wrapper on the porch, "Um, this is more Oswald's home than any of ours. So why don't we all cool off and meet here on the front porch in, say, half an hour?"

Oswald exhaled. He hadn't realized he had been holding his breath. "Thank you, Tiny. Yes, let's all reconvene here in thirty minutes. Reggie, you go get that credit card, and Mo, can you get Pixie to come around, too?"

"Thanks for agreeing to meet. And I am sorry I scared you. I guess I'm learning a lot, including about myself, and, well, it's not always nice," Oz said. The others listened.

"This *all* has to stop. There are stains everywhere from spilled food, squirted ketchup—"

Tiny raised his paw. "My bad. I'll clean those stains for sure."

"Thanks for accepting responsibility, Tiny. You're setting a good precedent," Oz said.

"Tiny's our president?" Pixie said. Her glasses threw reflections around the porch.

"Pardon me?" Oz said. Hazel started to chuckle, then Reggie and Tessa, and soon everyone was laughing. At Pixie. A storm brewed in her face. She gnashed her teeth.

Oz clinked a spoon against a mug. "Hold on, everyone. Pixie, I know what it feels like to be the butt of a joke."

"I know you all think I'm dull and clumsy. I know none of you like me very much." Pixie started to cry.

"Don't be silly," Tessa tried to comfort her. Oz decided it was better to be honest.

"You have to admit we didn't meet under the best circumstances. I think you need to be realistic, Pixie," Oswald said. "It will take a while before we all know how much of our unfortunate introduction was down to eyesight—"

Pixie's crying turned into wailing. She waved her large body back and forth. She grabbed one of the raccoons and sobbed into his fur, then moved to the next.

"I'm *so* sorry. I didn't mean to do it." She flung that raccoon to the side then clutched Tessa to her, making her disappear in her brown furry mass. Pixie continued to sob. "I didn't know she was in there. I thought I was helping."

"What are you talking about?" Frank said.

Pixie slumped to the floor. "Esmeralda. I cooked Esmeralda. She must have fallen asleep in the pot, because when I went into the kitchen, I saw the big pot of chili on the stove with the lid off. I thought somebody had forgotten to cover it. I turned the burner on to heat the chili for the party. I was only trying to help . . . "

For a few minutes, no one said a thing. A car rolled down the quiet street. A woman walked her small dog.

"That's great news," Reggie said.

"What do you mean?" Pixie said.

"That it wasn't Miss Ann who almost cooked Esmeralda," Tiny said.

"They'll let her out of jail once you tell them you did it," Mo said.

Pixie jumped up, eyes wild, teeth bared. She flung her paw against her forehead and leaned against the chair as though she might faint. "I can't give myself up. What if they decide I'm a dangerous animal? A danger to the public? They could . . . you know—" She let out a wail. "They could put me down!"

Everyone was quiet for another moment. The tweeting of the neighborhood birds contrasted with the serious conversation.

"You mean they can kill you, if they think you're violent?" Tessa asked.

It seemed most of the animals knew this to be a fact, given the uncomfortable nods and "uh-huhs."

"But this was an accident, an honest mistake. You didn't know anyone was in the pot," Oz said.

"An 'honest' mistake?" Pixie said. "That would make me an honest groundhog?"

"That's right," Frank added. "Like Oz said, it was an accident. No one would ever think there was an animal in a pot of veggie chili."

"You didn't see her in there?" Mo said.

"No. Truly, I didn't," Pixie said.

A lawnmower buzzed in the distance.

"I have an idea," Oz said. They all looked at him. "You know how they black out people's faces and change their voices on TV sometimes? To protect their identity?" It seemed most of them knew what he was talking about.

Oz continued, "Melvin knows how to operate a video camera, and he's good on the computer. If he's willing to help, what if we make a video? Then we could send it to the police, to Animal Control, the press—the humans who can do something about it. That could get Miss Ann out. And we could protect Pixie's identity."

"I don't know about all this," Pixie said. "Wait, you said a video, right?"

They all nodded.

"Would it be on YouTube?"

Oswald looked at Tiny, who nodded. "Well, I don't see why not," Oswald said.

"OK, then. I'll do it."

36

NO DOUBT

Wednesday was the next day Joey could go to the animal sanctuary, because Ms. Harris didn't work that Tuesday. Joey wore plenty of bug repellent and the mosquitoes mostly left him alone. Ms. Harris pushed the rickshaw toward Naja's building.

"Hop in. I'll drive." Ms. Harris grinned.

"You sure? I'm kind of heavy," Joey said.

Ms. Harris laughed. "You're a regular bean pole. Come on." Joey got in, and Ms. Harris pedaled the rickshaw over to the flock disorder unit. They were chatting and laughing as they walked in.

"Hi, Joey, Ms. Harris. Glad to see you—honk," Naja said. She flapped her wings. Joey opened the gate to her pen and walked in without asking Ms. Harris. He crouched down and Naja waddled up to him, resting her neck across his shoulder. He ran his hand down her smooth back feathers, breathing in the smell of her, like dust and sun.

"Hey, Naja." He smiled. She was definitely getting better.

Joey stood up and bird and boy walked out, then Joey and Ms. Harris helped Naja into the rickshaw.

"Glad someone gets to have fun around here." She smiled and left for her office.

Joey pedaled his goose friend down the path away from the building, clattering a rhythm of wheels against the boards. They came out of the shade into an open area of grassland with

183

the Patuxent River in the distance. A path cut across the field on a diagonal. Naja started flapping extra hard.

"OK, girl. Give me a minute, let me get up to speed," Joey said.

Joey pedaled as he counted, and Naja honked. She flapped, took large, full strokes, and launched. Joey pumped as fast as he could. Naja glided for a moment then landed back on the rickshaw. They did this twice more. Then Naja said, "I'd like to try taking off from the ground." Joey brought the rickshaw to a stop.

"OK."

"You know, like a regular goose." She looked excited.

"What should I do?" Joey was a little nervous, but he didn't know why.

"You've already done so much for me. Thank you," Naja said. She ran, honked, ran a few more steps, and then took off. Her strokes were quick and strong with the tips of her wings coming into the middle her chest. Her long black neck stretched out. She paddled her webbed feet with each beat of her wings.

She gained height, her strokes became smaller, and she glided. She was headed toward the break in the trees.

"I'll wait here," Joey yelled, but Naja had already flown through the trees, over the river, and away.

"What's going on? Is he OK?" Carlton asked Ms. Harris. Joey pedaled the rickshaw in circles about fifty yards from Carlton's car.

"Naja left a little while ago," Ms. Harris said.

"Naja?" Carlton said.

"That goose he'd been helping."

"Oh, right. Sorry," Carlton said, rubbing his forehead. "It's been a lot going on for all of us, especially for Joey."

"I know. Joey did a great job with that goose. He's the one that got her to fly again." Ms. Harris paused, looked at Joey still riding in circles. "It's hard rehabbing animals. You go through a lot with them, and when it works—you say good-bye." They both watched Joey pedaling for a moment.

Carlton offered his hand. "We want to thank you for all you've done for Joey. Helping him with his school project, placing Naja at his mom's house . . . "

"How's that going? Any news? None of us can imagine Ann doing anything like that," Ms. Harris said.

"I know. None of us can. But the district attorney is under a lot of pressure from animal groups after it hit the newspapers. What bad luck—a newspaper photographer being right there." Carlton shook his head.

"They're keeping her in jail until the hearing. They want to 'send a message,' that sort of thing. Well, anyway. Thanks again. Joey's going to miss coming here. He talks about wanting to be like you when he grows up," Carlton said.

Ms. Harris laughed. "That's a first. It's been a real pleasure working with your son. He's a fine young man. He doesn't have to stop coming, you know. There's plenty he can do. You're all always welcome."

"Maybe when all this clears up. That would be nice."

Joey slammed the car door. His dad didn't say a thing, he just waved to Ms. Harris as they drove down the long drive, surrounded by fields and trees too thick to see through. Carlton rolled the windows down. The smell of green and river and dusk washed over them.

"Hey, we have jerk chicken tonight with plantains and everything," Carlton said.

Joey stared out the window.

"What for? Is this a good-bye dinner? You sending me away?"

"Joey! What would ever make you think a thing like that?"

"Everybody else leaves. First you, then Bradyn moves away. Mom made Oswald leave. Then she goes. Now Naja. . . . That's it—no more friends with animals *or* people for me. Not worth it." He promised himself he wouldn't cry, but that wasn't working out so well.

"Oh, Joey—you can't let that stop you. It's just life, son," Carlton said while taking quick glances at him as they drove past more trees, then fields, with a few houses and barns. "I know it's hard."

"I didn't know there were this many farms out here," Joey said.

"Dang, with what you three kids eat—you keep at least five of them in business." Carlton looked over to Joey, who laughed despite that being another thing he'd promised not to do. He'd wanted to stay mad at his dad for letting his mom throw him out all those years ago. They passed through more woods before they got to the end of St. Thomas Church Road and turned right.

"Mom goes a different way," Joey said.

"Does she now?" Carlton raised an eyebrow.

"Yeah, past the high school."

"Oh. That's where your mother and I went."

They turned left onto Duley Station Road. More trees and houses.

"How come you let her throw you out?" Joey said.

"Let who throw me out?"

"Mom."

The road turned left. More farms.

"Now, Joey. We've been through this."

"If you were a real man, you wouldn't have let her do that. I'm just saying." Joey was surprised at his brashness. But he'd wanted to ask this for a long time.

"So that's what you think. All right then." Carlton pursed his lips, stared straight ahead. They turned right past Mattaponi Elementary School.

"Is that where you and mom went, too?"

"Your mom did, but my family—if you could call it that—didn't move here until I was in junior high."

"What do you mean about your family?" Joey looked at his dad. He never heard him talk like that.

More curves in the road, more stretches of trees punctuated by houses.

"My mom and dad didn't want to be together. They hooked up when they were real young. Too young. Kind of like your mom and me."

"So?"

"Well, for my folks, they thought staying together for the kids was the right thing. But we saw nothing but fussing, and arguing, and hurt between them, for years. Man, back then I'd do anything to get out of that house." Carlton paused while he turned onto the highway. "Like I said, your mom and I, we met in high school. We were just too young to know what we wanted. That's what happened between me and your mom. She didn't kick me out."

"It wasn't because you liked Suzette?"

His dad didn't say anything for a minute. They turned right onto Trumps Hill Road. "Whatever you want to think, Joey, I wish you'd stop blaming Suzette. If I hadn't found her, I'd have met someone else. No doubt."

Joey was quiet during dinner. If it hadn't been Suzette, it would have been someone else, 'no doubt.' He watched Noah and Mary. Noah reminded him of a chubbier version of himself. And Mary was smart. She asked good questions and always wanted to know how things worked.

After dinner, Joey helped clear the table, then was excused. He went on the computer in the family room as usual, did some homework, and uploaded it. From where he was sitting, he could hear Suzette and his dad's conversation.

"Oh, poor little guy. He was attached to that goose. Good for the goose, of course. Why couldn't she stay around these parts?" Suzette said.

"You're asking the wrong guy—I don't know anything about geese," his dad said. They dried the pots and pans and put them away.

"There's been so much change. What do you say we go over to Ann's on Saturday? Let Joey have some time with his cat—what's it called? Marvin?" Suzette said.

"Melvin."

"OK, Melvin. And I could give the house a once-over—keep it straight for when Ann gets back. You could mow the grass. Noah and Mary could play in the yard—it's fenced in," Suzette said.

"I don't know. I've got enough to do over here without getting involved in all that . . . "

"Come on. It's for Joey."

37

VIDEO

Oswald charged up the steps to the Edwardses' porch on Thursday morning. "Ready?" he said to Melvin and Zola. They looked like they were, both sitting at attention, a red bow tie in Zola's mouth.

"Mr. Edwards said Tiny could borrow it," Melvin said.

"Excellent choice, excellent," Oswald said. His tail made curlicues in the air. "Please thank him for me. We'd best be going." Oswald turned down the steps with Melvin and Zola in tow. Today was the video shoot.

It had taken two days for the animals to agree to a plan and to gather everything they needed. They'd decided on a two-part video: a re-enactment of what happened, and Pixie's confession. Oswald would direct and narrate—explain to the viewers what they were about to see and what they just saw, that sort of thing. And of course, he would do the reenactment of Esmeralda getting into the pot of chili. Tiny would interview Pixie for the confession. Melvin would shoot the video and edit it on the computer afterward. During the editing, Oswald and Melvin would put subtitles in for the majority of people who don't understand Animal. And Zola would help with security—help Oswald keep control, although all the animals wanted to make this work.

Then yesterday they got some good news. Before they would go ahead with the video, they wanted to find out how

Esmeralda was. "I'd feel funny re-enacting the accident, if you know . . . ," Tessa had said. The animals agreed and asked Mrs. Edwards if she wouldn't mind finding out for them.

"It's good news, everyone," Mrs. Edwards told them all on Ann's porch. "Esmeralda is doing well. She's not hurt, although she is suffering from some post-traumatic stress."

Zola sat up. "Maybe I could help?" Mrs. Edwards patted her head. "Exactly. They've agreed to let Esmeralda finish her recovery at our house, hopefully in a few days."

That let them schedule the video shoot for this morning. Oswald, Melvin, and Zola went into Ann's house and joined the rest of the animals gathered in the dining room. They all sat attentively. Oswald reached for his clipboard, a lid from one of the takeout meals they shouldn't have ordered off of Ann's credit card. He kept it as a reminder. He checked items off as Tessa and Reggie scampered around to confirm they had them. Video camera, extension cords, extra lamps, a work glove with two holes cut in it, and a set of magic markers because Pixie had insisted on makeup even though her face would be covered with the work glove. It looked like everything was there.

"OK, we're ready to shoot the re-enactment. Everyone into the kitchen, please," Oswald said. Tiny and Mo held the video camera steady on top of an overturned pot on the kitchen table. Melvin looked at the viewfinder screen and pressed different buttons. Oswald climbed onto the counter, using a chair the raccoons had pushed into place for him.

"Melvin, can you pan the camera across the room—see if you can get everything you need?" Oswald said.

"Sure thing, boss," Melvin said without any sarcasm. Frank perched on top of a cabinet, and the rest of the animals clustered by the doorway around Pixie.

"OK, Frank, you'll take over for this next shot."

"Got it," Frank said.

Oswald climbed into the pot. The lid was on the counter. There was nothing in the pot this time, and they checked three times to make sure the burners were off.

"Frank will count us in for this scene. OK—here we go!" Oswald ducked down in the pot.

Frank called out, "Places, everyone. Melvin, start shooting in three, two, one, and we're rolling . . . "

Pixie walked into the kitchen wearing the large garden glove over her head. The fingers stuck up in the air. Tessa and Reggie had gnawed the eyeholes in it so Pixie could see out. Her sparkly eyeglasses were placed over the glove, because they wouldn't fit underneath. She hummed as she looked around the kitchen, put an apron on that she'd rolled up, then looked right into the camera.

"Hi. I'm Pixie Groundhog, from Barnard Hill Park and—"

"Cut!" Oswald popped his head above the rim. "Pixie, you said you wanted to be anonymous. You don't want anyone to know who you are until you know what will happen to you. Remember?"

"Right, right. Sorry."

Oswald ducked back down into the pot.

Frank said, "Take two. Three, two, one—action!"

"Hi, I'm Pixie Groundhog, and my ex-husband is Grape-juice. Grape, if you're listening, I want you to know that I love you and want you to come back—"

"Cut." Oswald popped up again.

Melvin looked out from the camera. "I can redo the audio in the editing, so we can take out the things she shouldn't be saying and you could narrate anything else the viewer needs to know. You're doing the overall narration, anyway."

"Good idea, Melvin. I like it. OK—Frank, take it away." Oswald disappeared into the pot again.

Melvin returned to operating the video camera, and Frank counted them in. They let Pixie ramble on, knowing Melvin would edit it out. All the animals watched the playback.

"That's fine. Plenty for me to work with," Melvin said.

They took a short break outside before all of them except Reggie, Tessa, and Chuck came back in to help film the confession. Pixie sat at the end of the couch so that a framed picture of Joey and his mother was visible on the side table. Mo and Tiny dragged two extra lamps into the living room under

Oswald's instructions. The two raccoons moved them around until Oswald was satisfied with the lighting. Tiny put on the bow tie. He sat on the coffee table to do the interview.

As soon as Oswald counted them in, Pixie spilled her groundhog guts. She cried and begged forgiveness. She couldn't stop herself from mentioning her name and begging Grapejuice to return. But rather than stopping the video, Oswald waddled up to Melvin and whispered, "Just bleep those words out, too." Melvin nodded and the filming continued.

By the time they finished, it was dinnertime.

"Thank you, everyone. I could never have done this without any one of you. As a small thank-you, I've asked Chuck, Reggie, and Tessa to organize dinner on the back deck. So please, everyone, enjoy."

The animals thundered out of the enlarged cat-flap hole to the deck where there was a wonderful array of bits of fried fish, French fries, pizza crusts, Chinese noodles, watermelon rinds, cookies, and lots of other things. It was organized into neat rows with the top of a pineapple in the center for decoration. Oswald didn't remember ever having such a nice dinner with friends before. They told jokes, talked about how the day went, and took turns trying on Pixie's red-glove disguise.

The temperature dropped as the rays of the setting sun gave a last grab at the day.

"Goodnight, guys, I'm off. You coming, Melvin?" Zola said.

"No, I'm good. I'll stay here tonight. Tell the Edwards for me?" Melvin said.

"Sure," the large dog said and wandered off toward home.

"I'm off too—I need to stretch my wings. See you all tomorrow." Frank hopped onto the deck railing and took flight. The strong beating of his wings made a rhythmic swooshing until he blended in with the darkening sky.

After cleaning up from dinner, the rest of them moseyed back inside. Tessa, Reggie, and Hazel went upstairs to their nests. Pixie curled up on the chair in the living room. Tiny, Mo, and Chuck shared the couch, but now with an old sheet on it to protect it.

Melvin went toward the stairs. "I'm going to sleep on Joey's bed. I miss him."

"I know. So do I." Oswald paused, looked around. "Melvin, I can't thank you enough. If it wasn't for you, I don't think we could have—"

"Fuggedaboutit. We'll do the narration and stuff in the morning. Then we can send it off." Melvin disappeared up the stairs.

Oswald curled up in the big comfy chair in the study and fell asleep happier than he'd ever been before.

38

TERRIBLE BUT NOT TRAGIC

The animals clustered in the study and stared at the computer screen. It had taken all morning and into the afternoon to record Oswald's narration and do the editing. Melvin and Oswald would do the subtitles once everyone agreed on the final edit. Oswald was grateful and impressed with Melvin's skills and patience.

"Melvin, go ahead," Oswald said. Melvin clicked the mouse and the video played.

The shot faded in with Oswald on the couch.

"Hello. I'm Oswald Opossum, and I am honored to introduce you to a young groundhog, a brave and good-hearted critter. She will remain anonymous in this video for reasons that will soon become clear. She is here today to explain what happened this past Sunday at 3103 Perry Street, Mount Rainier, Maryland—a terrible but not tragic mistake that led to the wrongful arrest and jailing of Ms. Ann Jones. Ms. Groundhog is here today to set the record straight. We hope this will free Ms. Jones and reunite her with her ten-year-old son." Oswald turned to the picture of Ann and Joey on the table next to the couch and Melvin zoomed in on it.

Next was the re-enactment. The animals were engrossed, yelling at the computer screen, trying to warn Pixie that Oswald was in the pot, seeming to forget that it was all make-believe this time. Oswald hoped this meant the video was good—that it was convincing.

Melvin had done an excellent job of removing Pixie's self-identifying words. The result was awkward at times, but they decided this made the video seem all the more real. The only thing left to do was the subtitles.

When it was over, Oswald looked around the room. There wasn't a dry eye in the house. *Maybe this will work.*

There was the sound of the key in the front door and voices—Joey's and someone else's.

"Quick—everyone out, now!" Oswald whisper-shouted. He shut down the video and computer. Tiny and Melvin herded everyone out the back onto the deck. "You can stay, of course," Oswald quickly said to Melvin before leaving, not that he needed to.

Oswald lingered, looking through the glass French doors while the other animals ran, leapt, and flew off the deck and scattered.

"Hey, Melvin, my main cat!" Joey said. He radiated happiness at the sight of his cat. Melvin purred and butted his head against the boy. Cat and boy, Oswald could see and feel the bond. A chill rolled through Oswald. He *was* glad Joey had such a good pal in Melvin, but realized he didn't have that with Joey anymore—now that he'd ruined it. Or with anybody else for that matter.

A woman—this must be Joey's stepmom, Suzette—looked around, picked things up, and shook her head. Two little kids, a girl and a boy, wandered around. *Must be his stepsiblings. They look nice too—another whole family for Joey. He really doesn't need me.* Oswald slunk down the steps and under the deck to his room.

❖ ❖ ❖

"What's all this?" Suzette walked around. There were extension cords, lamps, pillows, magic markers, mugs, and all sorts of things all over.

"Hey, can I show Noah and Mary my old toys in the garage?" Joey said. He thought this might be a good distraction from the mess in the house. Though he couldn't explain it, he had his suspicions. He looked at Melvin, who nodded to say, *tell you outside.*

"Good idea," Suzette said. "Don't let them get near that pool. I see it's still up. I'll get started in here."

Joey and Melvin went out the door to the deck.

Mary and Noah ran back and forth the width of the deck, pretending to be airplanes. Joey shut the door.

"What the heck is going on? The place is a mess. And what happened to the cat flap? It's just a big hole in the door now," Joey whispered.

"You know, you could warn a cat, man," Melvin said. "We were in the middle of videoing something. Sorry about the flap—made it bigger so everyone could get in and out OK."

"Making a video? I was going to Skype or email you tonight. We were supposed to come tomorrow. But when Suzette picked me up from school today she told me there was a change of plans," Joey said.

Noah zoomed by, arms outstretched, making airplane noises, heading for the steps. Joey caught him round the waist. "Whoa there, little man, let's go see what toys we can find." Joey led his little brother and sister to the garage. They emerged with balls, a scooter, and a small bike.

The sound of Joey's dad's car door closing filtered to the backyard. A few minutes later he emerged on the back deck. "Hi, kids."

Mary, on the small bike, and Noah, on the scooter, circled around Carlton.

"Is your mom's mower in the garage?" Carlton said.

"As far as I know," Joey said.

"I can watch Mary and Noah while I mow. Why don't you go in and give Suzette a hand inside. She says it's like a bunch of animals had been in there."

A couple of hours later and after fried fish dinners from Rhode Island Avenue, they got ready to head back to Joey's dad's house.

"The place looks great—all ready for me and mom," Joey said. His dad and Suzette didn't say anything.

"I'm going to go over to the neighbors' house. The Edwards, right? I brought them a little thank-you for taking care of Melvin," Suzette said. "Joey, do you want to come along—introduce us?"

"That's a good idea. You two do that, while I pack up the computer. That way you can use it as much as you want at home, Joey, instead of us all trying to use the one in the family room," Carlton said.

"MEOW!" Melvin made lots of odd noises.

"Is he going to be sick?" Suzette said. She made a face. Then Melvin started making sounds like he *was* going to throw up.

Joey ushered Melvin out the back door and down the steps to the grass.

"We gotta talk," Melvin said. "You *can't* take the computer. We haven't put the subtitles on the video yet. It's important so all humans can understand it."

"So what's this big important video about? Oswald trying to get famous again?" Joey said.

"No, I mean Oswald made the video—it was his idea, directed it. But it's not *about* him," Melvin spoke in hushed hurried tones while glancing over his shoulder. "I didn't want to tell you before, in case it doesn't work out."

"In case what doesn't work out?" Joey said.

"We're hoping the video will get your mom out of jail."

Joey's eyes got big.

Suzette popped her head out of the back door. Melvin made a few fake retching sounds.

"Poor thing. That's OK, then. I'll go over to the Edwardses' on my own," she said.

"Thanks, Suzette. I better stay with Melvin. Hope we don't have to take him to the vet," Joey said. Suzette left.

"It was the groundhog that did it. The possum was already in the pot of chili. The groundhog didn't know she was in there—she just put the lid on the pot and turned on the burner. And the rest, you know," Melvin said.

"For real? I'll go tell Dad and Suzette." He rocketed back into the house and spilled the story to his dad, who he was coiling the cables up.

"Well, that's really cute and everything, but we've all—your mom's family, and I chipped in, too—we've already hired a lawyer. They're putting together her case as it is. They're talking to the DA," Carlton said as he unplugged the screen from the computer and wound up more cords.

"But *Dad*, there's a confession and everything by the person who really did it!"

Carlton stood up and stopped what he was doing, "Really? Who's that?"

"It was Pixie, the groundhog—"

Carlton shook his head and sighed, "Oh, Joey. A groundhog? You know your mother talked to me about this, about your being so animal crazy. I mean, I didn't really see a problem, but now, I'm thinking she might be right."

"But *Daad*!" Joey promised the universe that if he could convince his dad of this one thing, he wouldn't try for anything else for a really long time—maybe not until he was eleven. But nothing worked. His dad was convinced sending a video confession by a groundhog would only make them seem like "a bunch of fools." And that they "should really let the professionals do their job and not meddle with the case." *Boy, grown-ups are dumb sometimes,* Joey thought.

"Joey, will you please control your cat? This is the third time he's jumped in the car," Carlton said. He lifted Melvin out and put him down less gently than the first two times.

"Noah, Mary, hop in. Let me buckle you up," Suzette said. Mary hopped in and did up the belts on her car seat. Noah took off laughing. His mom gave chase. Melvin wiggled through Suzette's legs, under the car, and slinked in on the floor of the front seat.

"Got you!" Carlton said, grabbing the back end of the cat and tugged. "What's with you, cat?"

"Joey, get in and close the door." Suzette was still chasing Noah. Now was Joey's chance. He whispered to Mary, "I need to get Melvin back to your house." She nodded. "I'll think up a reason we *have* to go back to my house. I might need you to play along. OK?"

"Should I tell Noah?" Mary said.

"No, this is big kid stuff. Just between you and me. OK?" Joey said. Mary nodded again then gestured to her left. The door opened and Suzette deposited a squirming, laughing Noah. Mary helped buckle him in.

Carlton put Melvin inside the front door of the house, closed it, and ran to the car. They were pulling away by the time Melvin had made it out the cat flap hole in the back and around the house.

When they turned onto Bladensburg Road, Joey said, "Oh no. I forgot my mom's old Twister game. I'm sorry, Mary, I know I promised to bring it."

"You FORGOT!? But you *promised,*" Mary said.

"That was a nice idea, Joey. We'll get it next time," Suzette said.

"But you promised!" Mary said.

Joey looked at her out of the corner of his eye and touched the skin below his eye. Mary started to cry.

"You know the waterworks don't work on me," Carlton said, making eye contact through the rearview mirror. Her pretend tears turned into pretend sniffles. Then in the meekest, sweetest voice she said, "That's all right, Daddy. I understand."

"Thanks, baby girl. That's my angel," Carlton said.

A moment later, Mary gave a long, sad sigh, in her highest, sweetest voice. A moment later, another. When she started the third, the turn signal went on.

"We're not that far. Saves me from coming back another day," Carlton said.

Suzette laughed. She held up her hand and made circles around her pinky. "Wrapped around, and around, and—"

Noah joined in, "Round and round and . . . "

39

THE POSSUM'S ALL RIGHT

"Won't be long," Joey said. He ran through the door of his mother's house and up the stairs.

"Psst. Melvin?"

"Right here. Great work, kid. What's the plan?" Melvin said.

Joey rummaged around in his closet and found a duffle bag. He ran to his mother's room and came back with the Twister game.

"Get in. You'll have to hide. And Suzette says she's allergic. Ready?"

"Don't forget to act like the bag isn't heavy, and don't let anyone else carry it."

"I'm not stupid," Joey said, zipped the bag, and took it downstairs.

"You should be all set," Joey's dad said as he plugged the mouse into the computer, moved it, and watched the screen. He looked at his watch. "It's not that late, if you want to watch TV downstairs with us."

Joey yawned. "That's OK. I'm kind of tired. I think I'll hang out here," he said.

"OK, son. Goodnight," his father said. He stopped at the door. "I'm sorry about all this, you know."

"I know."

"You know I love . . . we all love having you here. You can stay anytime. I'm just sorry it had to be for these reasons," his dad said.

"Yeah. It's fun."

"Really?"

"Yeah, really," Joey said.

His dad smiled. "Good. Good to know. Well, goodnight."

"Goodnight, Dad."

"You know, if you want to talk some more . . . " his dad said.

"Yeah, I know. I'm cool. I'll probably want to talk another time," Joey said.

"OK then," his dad said and finally left.

Joey waited for a few minutes then fired up the computer, slid his closet door open, and unzipped the bag.

"That took long enough!" Melvin said. He lay on the carpet and panted. "I don't feel so hot, man."

Joey opened the window and leaned out, looked around, and came back in. "Here, get some fresh air. There's a roof out here and a tree next to it. Should work for getting up and down."

Melvin jumped into the open window and hurried across the roof. A branch swayed and leaves rustled.

Joey waited at the window for Melvin. After five minutes he began to wonder where the cat could have gone. After ten, he started to worry. There was a soft knock at his door. "Joey, it's me—Mary," came a whisper. *Like there's another six-year-old girl in the house.* He let her in. She struggled to drag her bunny-shaped pajama bag into the room.

"He's in here," Mary said and plopped it on the floor. "He's heavy."

Joey loosened the pull cord. Melvin came out. "Big house. Wrong window. Could happen to anybody," Melvin said.

"You understand what he's saying?" Mary said.

"Yeah, I always could. You might when you're older."

Mary shrugged. "Maybe. Noah understands animals. Hey, do you want to play Twister?"

"It's too late. How about tomorrow?" Joey said.

Mary's eyes narrowed. "Mom's allergic to cats."

"Come on, I know you're cooler than that. I promise I'll play two games of whatever you want tomorrow if you keep quiet."

Mary thought for a moment, agreed, and skipped back to her room.

Joey locked his door, even though he wasn't supposed to; getting yelled at was a risk worth taking. Then he and Melvin worked together to put the subtitles on the video. It was faster with Joey's typing.

"Wow—that is really something. I *knew* she didn't do it, but this . . . " Joey said when they finished. He got up from the computer and paced back and forth across the room. "This is wild. I mean, this has *got* to do it. They should let my mom out the minute, no, *the second* they see this."

"The *micro*-second!" Melvin added.

Joey stopped in his tracks. "My dad's *got* to see this—then he'll believe it." Joey paced some more.

Melvin tilted his head, "I don't know—"

"What do you mean? How could he *not* believe it—and then send it to the police and court and stuff?" Joey said.

"I don't know, Joey. He might still not believe it, and then worse—call anyone we send it to and apologize for his 'over-enthusiastic son', blah, blah, blah. I mean, I could just hear him, 'I certainly hope this doesn't interfere with the case.' You know what grown-ups are like."

Joey plunked down on his bed. "Yeah. I guess you're right."

The two sat there for a moment staring at the dark window, unable to see what lay beyond. Joey gave a deep sigh.

"OK, we'll just do it, then." Joey thought for a minute, then continued, "So *Oswald* did this? It was his idea?"

Melvin was already tapping on the keyboard. "Yeah, the possum's all right." There were a few more keystrokes. "There—it's on YouTube." Joey looked over Melvin's shoulder.

"Hey, you're a lot quicker on the keyboard. Would you send the link out? Here's our list," Melvin asked, opening an email.

"Are you kidding? Of course!" Joey sent the email to everyone on the list the animals had made—the police department, the *Washington Post*, and Prince George's County Animal Control—with the YouTube link and contact details for "Mr. Oswald Opossum, representative of Ms. Groundhog."

After that they tried to go to sleep, with Melvin under the bed and Joey lying awake, mind whirring, stunned and hopeful.

40

THE NEED TO LEAVE

"I think that about covers it, Mr. Oswald," Detective Bonita Lavender said. She wore a gray pantsuit and a purple blouse. She clicked her briefcase shut. "If your client did this, like she says in the video, this could free Ms. Ann Jones. I'll talk to the district attorney."

"And I'll take this back to our office," the Animal Control officer said. The officer came with the detective, to interpret for the detective as well as to represent Animal Control, given Pixie's concerns about being labeled a dangerous animal. "I'll see what sort of immunity they might be willing to provide in return for her testimony. I agree—if it really happened like you show in the video, it certainly looks like an accident."

Oswald stood up on the couch and extended a paw. There were two mugs and a bowl of coffee on the table. It was a dull, drizzly Saturday.

"Thank you, Detective, Officer, for your time and for taking us seriously. My client understands what's at stake here— the conviction of an innocent woman."

Detective Lavender paused at the door. "I'll stop by to tell you as soon as we know. Hopefully tomorrow."

Oswald saw them out.

Frank, Reggie, Tessa, Hazel, Chuck, Mo, Tiny, and, of course, Pixie waited in the study. Oswald was met by a chorus of questions. He explained everything Detective Lavender told him. After much discussion and some confusion, they all agreed on one thing—there was nothing to do but wait.

The rain and the waiting stretched Saturday out. They watched movies, went out for food, bickered, and napped. Oswald kept reminding them to keep everything neat this time, in case Miss Ann did come home soon. Reggie's collecting was getting worse. He'd brought back all sorts of odds and ends he found outside—a doll's head, bottle tops, and a couple of LEGOs. "As long as you keep it neat and tidy." Oswald could see his collecting got worse when he was nervous.

Sunday morning, they heard a knock at the door. Mo and Tiny managed to open it. The rest of the animals scuttled into the study or out the cat flap hole, too nervous to face the detective.

"Hi, it's Detective Lavender, and the Animal Control officer from yesterday," Ms. Lavender said.

"Yes, yes, do come in," Mo said, still on Tiny's shoulders, then jumped down.

"Nice to see you, Detective, Officer. I'll go get Oswald," Tiny said then loped into the back of the house. There was the sound of animal voices and nails scrabbling.

Oswald walked into the living room. "Good to see you both, Detective, Officer. Can I get you some coffee?" But he didn't wait for an answer. "Mo, Chuck, could you get us coffee, please?" Oswald said.

Sounds of crockery clinking, water sloshing, and raccoons fussing came from the kitchen. Oswald smiled and drummed his digits on the coffee table. As much as he was bursting to hear what they had to say, part of him was also putting it off, in case it was bad news. A moment later, Chuck pulled and Mo pushed a skateboard into the living room with two mugs of coffee sloshing on top.

"Thank you," the Animal Control officer said. Detective Lavender smiled and took out a folder. Oswald held his breath.

The Animal Control officer spoke, "We think we have a good deal for Ms. X. If she agrees to give the police a statement in person, and her statement is found to be true, we cannot anticipate any reason to detain her."

"That does sound fair. But can you tell me what you mean by 'cannot anticipate'? You might still have to keep her—as a 'dangerous animal'?" Oswald said. He swallowed hard.

The Animal Control officer leaned forward. "I don't think it's anything to worry about. I just can't say absolutely, one hundred percent, what the outcome will be until we go through it all. Say if she went wild during the interview and bit someone—that sort of thing."

"Yes, yes. I do understand," Oswald said and jumped off the couch. "This is terrific news! Let me go get her."

He raced through the house and out the cat flap hole. "They agreed—the deal's on!" Oswald stood panting, looking at all the animals gathered on the deck. "Where is she?"

The animals were quiet.

"She said she had to go to the bathroom," Simone said.

Tiny cleared his throat. "She didn't come back—Pixie's gone."

41

TO SEE A MONDAY

"Joey, are you sure you're well enough to go to school?" Suzette peered out the minivan window. She had that worried-mom look on her face. The back seat was empty. They had dropped off Noah and Mary first. He stood next to the car. *Don't go all gooey stepmom on me now of all times.* He tried not to show the strain of carrying an extra fourteen pounds in his knapsack.

His explanation for not seeming right this morning, a slight stomachache, was backfiring. He needed a reason for the expressions he must have been making from the effort of carrying his knapsack with Melvin inside. At least for Suzette, who seemed to notice everything the way his mother did. *Jeez, do you all have a worry gene or something?*

He loved having Melvin at his dad's house over the weekend, and Mary was cool with it, but it had been nerve-racking. Mary snuck him food, although it was mostly peanut butter sandwiches. Now, Noah, he was hard work. Got into everything and nearly discovered Melvin more than once. Joey wondered if he was such a pain when he was little. He'd ask his mom when she was back home.

That was another thing. Every time he thought about his mom, and he was surprised how often that was, he felt kind of sick. *Oh man, I'm nothing but a big old baby about this.*

Although Joey liked school for the most part, he was never as glad to see a Monday before. He and Melvin had worked out a plan. Melvin would hide in Joey's knapsack, and Joey would let him out near school. Melvin would walk home. He'd made that trip lots of times when he used to walk Joey to school. As far as the Edwards were concerned, they would probably just think they hadn't seen Melvin for a few days. Nothing out of the ordinary for a cat. Joey was dying to know if Oswald had heard anything from the police yet.

Suzette drove off. Joey waved and smiled. *Finally.* After she turned a corner, Joey crossed the street where there was a house with a low brick wall around the yard. He put his knapsack on it, unzipped it, and pretended he was looking for something. Melvin hopped out and sat there like he'd been there all along.

"Hey, doc!" It was Ghalib. He swung his leg off his bike and glided to a stop. "I see your cat came with you—cool."

"Oh, right. He just came up to say hi before school, with me living at my dad's and all." Joey said.

"That's real decent." Ghalib nodded and looked at Melvin as though he saw him in a new way. "Hey, any news about your mom?"

Joey felt like he'd been punched in the stomach. Kids kept asking him about his mom. He knew they meant well. Or at least most of them did. Ghalib did.

"Nah, nothing yet," Joey managed.

"Sorry, man," Ghalib said. He looked glum, then brightened, and gave Joey a friendly thwack on the arm. "I'm sure she'll be back real soon, driving you nuts like moms do." He grinned. "Catch you later." He rolled his bike across the street toward school.

"He seems all right," Melvin said.

Joey looked across the street at everyone going into the school. "Yeah. I guess."

"Go on, you better go before the bell rings. I'll come by in the mornings before school, so we can catch up," Melvin said. He turned to leave.

Joey got that nervous feeling in his gut—he didn't want to part with Melvin. But he also thought that was kind of babyish. He kicked a pebble. "Hey."

Melvin turned to face Joey.

"Thank Oswald for me, will ya?"

"Sure, man."

Joey had trouble concentrating in class. He was glad for lunch when he sat with Ria and her friends. None of them asked about his mom. He figured Ria told them not to. It was nice to have a breather. At recess, he shot hoops with Ghalib against a couple of the older boy's friends. A bonus of being tall for your age was that people liked you on their side.

The afternoon seemed endless. His teacher was telling them about the Mayan civilization. Usually he'd be interested. But he found himself counting the painted cinder blocks on the wall.

"Joseph Jones, please come to the front." Ms. Tinderclaw's voice barely made it into Joey's brain. She was standing by the door.

"Joey, are you with us?" she said.

"Yes, Ms. Tinderclaw. Yes, the Mayans. Sorry, what was the question?" Joey said. The class tittered.

She was using her kind, soft voice, so he wasn't in trouble. "No, Joey. Someone's here to see you. Come here, please. And bring your things, I think you'll be leaving school early today."

That got his adrenaline going—didn't sound good. She held the door open for him and he walked out into the hall with his heart thumping. When he saw his father in the hall waiting for him, it took all his strength not to burst into tears. "Uh-oh. Is it about Melvin? If it is, I'm really sorry. But he didn't mess anything up, I mean you didn't even—"

"Hang on a minute. Relax," his dad said.

Joey felt relieved, but when he looked at his father again, he could see he was emotional, too. He'd only seen his dad get like that once, when his grandmother, Joey's great-grandmother, died. That sent another shot of fear through him.

"Is everyone OK? Mom? Suzette? Mary? Noah?" Joey said.

His dad put his arm around his shoulder and walked him down the hall. "Everyone's fine, son. Better than fine. Your mom's out of jail."

42

THE SECOND BEST NEWS

"I parked up at your mom's, easier to walk back," Joey's dad said as they left the school. But Joey couldn't go slow. He broke into a run.

"Be careful!" Joey's dad called out after him. He thought he heard his dad chuckle.

It was a nice day, but it wouldn't have mattered. There could have been a hurricane. The houses, trees, and people were a blur.

"Hi, Joey!" Mr. Edwards yelled from his porch. He never yelled. He was beaming and holding Zola back.

"She's back, Joey! She's back!" Zola barked.

"I know!" Joey bounded through the gate, up the porch steps, and through the front door. In two strides, he hug-attacked his mom. She'd had her back to the door as she'd been talking to a couple of people. He didn't care who saw him.

"Mom!"

His mother kissed the top of his head, "*You,* you, young man, are the thing I missed the most." She held him at arm's length and looked at him hard. "You're more handsome than I remember." There were tears streaming down her cheeks. Joey burst into sobs.

"Can you give us a minute, please?" she said to a man who looked familiar and a woman who went out onto the porch.

Joey realized the man was the photographer from the paper. But the other person was different—not the lady from before.

"The newspaper again?" Joey said.

"Yes, but they sent a different reporter. Not the lady who called in the animal incident."

Joey's dad tapped on the screen door. "Hi." He looked bashful. Joey had never seen him look like that before. In a flash, Joey wondered if he'd been a shy kid, too. He'd told Joey this enough times, but Joey thought he only said it to make him feel better.

"Hey, Carlton, come on in. How was our boy?" Ann said. "Was he any trouble?"

"Not at all. You know it's great having him around. You should have seen him with Mary—got on like a house on fire," Carlton said.

"Probably up to something, in my experience," she said and ruffled his hair again, but Joey didn't mind.

"I'll let you all settle in. I just wanted to say welcome home. Suzette will bring Joey's things and the computer back this afternoon, after she's picked up the kids."

"You want anything before you go—a cup of coffee? There might be sodas in the fridge," Ann said.

A TV truck pulled up in front of the house. A cameraman and a woman got out.

Ann looked stricken. She touched her hair. "Carlton, would you stall them? This is turning into a real zoo," she said.

"I can do that." Then to Joey, "Here's my cell, text Suzette and tell her I'll be here helping out." Joey took his dad's cell, texting as he walked out the back.

◆ ◆ ◆

"Hey Joey—my main *hu*-man!" Melvin rolled around on the warm deck.

Joey gave Melvin a rub. "Did Pixie talk to the cops? Did she give her statement?"

Zola's head popped over the fence. "She must have. But we don't know for sure."

Oswald popped out from under the deck. "Joey—*wonderful* to see you!" He started up the deck steps then stopped, looking unsure as to whether or not he was welcome. He cleared his throat, "Yes, yes. Well, it was all up in the air after, see, after Pixie ran off—too scared to talk to the police face-to-face was all we could surmise."

There was a commotion next to the garage. Grunting, leaves crunching, and branches snapping were followed by a green-and-yellow lampshade rolling out of the overgrowth.

Pixie lay spread-eagled, catching her breath. "I came back to tell y'all that I did it. I went to the police and made my statement."

"You did it then! It worked—my mom's home!" Joey spilled down the steps and ran toward Pixie and Oswald, arms spread for a group hug, a huge grin splitting his face. Oswald retreated under a bush, looking nervous at the prospect of physical contact. But Pixie ran toward Joey with her own toothy grin. After he let go of Pixie, he crouched down and looked at Oswald blinking out from the dense foliage.

"You gotta let me thank you. You saved my mom!"

Oswald crawled out and blinked up at Joey. "I did? I mean I did. Actually *we* did. It was a true team effort. There was Tiny and of course Frank did some of the directing, and—"

"Ah, my mom's got to hear all this. She's going to *love* it. She's starting to speak Animal now, too."

Oswald blinked some more. "So you think she wouldn't mind seeing me?"

"Mind? Are you crazy? Come on!"

As boy, possum, cat, and groundhog walked toward the front of the house, the raccoons—Tessa, Reggie, Hazel, Simone, and Frank—all came out of their various hiding places.

Miss Ann was sitting in one of the chairs on the porch, talking to the TV interviewer. The cameraman filmed and the photographer clicked away. The reporter recorded the interview on her phone.

The humans turned at the sound of paws, claws, and wings.

Miss Ann grinned. "And here they are. Let them tell you—it's their story."

She moved things to make more room. "Please, everyone come on up on the porch," she said.

The TV people told everyone where to sit. Joey's dad got more chairs from the deck. Joey and even Ann helped with animal translations. The interview took quite a while. There was a lot to tell.

By the time the media left, everyone was exhausted. Suzette came by with the kids and Joey's stuff. They ordered pizza for everyone, all beings. Carlton and Suzette carried Mary and Noah, who had fallen asleep, into their car and said their good-byes.

"You can stay home from school tomorrow if you want. Your dad told the school you might," his mother said.

And then the big news—the animals could stay.

"Oh wow, I knew you'd come around, Mom!" Joey said.

Pixie sat up, the lampshade jangling. "Ooh, I could dig a lovely burrow in the backyard. I could make it just like home, with a grass bed, and cubbyholes, and . . . " She stopped talking for a moment—looked wistful. "Actually, I think I may move back home, if that's all right—I do miss it."

"Of course," Ann said, "But do come by and visit us."

Then the raccoons started reminiscing about their den in the tree and how it always smelled like leaves and how it was the best sleeping place.

"I do miss our place, and our 120, or is it 122 relations?" Tessa said.

And soon all of them realized they wanted to go home to Barnard Hill Park. All of them except Oswald, of course, who was home. After promises to stay in touch, to have picnics in the park, visits at the house, and for Ann to let Pixie "touch up those roots," Joey, Ann, Oz, and Melvin waved as the animals walked down Perry Street, the rats on the raccoons' backs, and Frank flying off ahead.

"Please give our regards to Queenie the cat," Oswald called out as they left.

Oswald relaxed on the porch with Joey, Ann, and Melvin.

The Edwardses' screen door creaked open. Mrs. Edwards stepped out with Zola and another animal by her feet. She leaned against her porch railing. "Welcome home, Annie." Oswald had never heard her call her that before. "I just wanted to show you something. I mean *someone*." She pointed to the table where the second animal had jumped up—Esmeralda.

"Hi, everyone," was all she said, but she did seem to be smiling. Zola gave her a big lick down her back, nearly lifting her off the table.

Ann leaned back in the chair with Melvin in her lap and her hand on Joey's back. "That's the second-best sight I've seen in a long time."

"Isn't she, though?" Mrs. Edwards said. "She'll be staying here until she's fully recovered, with Zola's help obviously. Then it will be up to her if she wants to stay or go back to the park."

"What about Mr. Edwards? I thought he was against feeding grown wild animals?" Joey said.

"You're as surprised as I am. But I guess it's true, the only guarantee in this world is change." Mrs. Edwards smiled.

The Joneses' house phone started ringing again. It had hardly stopped since Ann got home.

"Hey, Oz—it's Oprah. She wants you on her show. . . . Hey, Oz, it's Ellen DeGeneres on the phone for you . . . " Joey said.

"Very funny," Oswald said. But their joking wasn't too far off. Everyone was interested in the story: woman wrongly jailed; animals make a confession video that goes viral and saves the day. There were loads of angles and everyone wanted one.

They put the phone on silent and let voice mail pick up.

43

A REAL CARD

The moment they turned the ringer back on the next day, the calls started again.

"I'll go get him," Joey said. He took the phone out back, down the steps, and stuck his head under the deck.

"It's for you, Oz."

Oswald poked his head out from his wooden-crate house. He blinked. "Joey, please. I do appreciate your sense of humor, but I am awfully tired," Oswald said.

Joey covered the mouthpiece. "No, for real. It's for you."

"All right, then," Oswald said and dragged himself out from under the deck.

Joey left the handset with Oz and went back in the house. It was about midday. A steady stream of friends, relatives, and the press had been calling since seven. His mother came up with a response for anyone calling for an interview: they thanked them for their interest and told them Ann would get back to them within a week, as she needed time with her family. They thought this sounded better than 'go away.'

Oswald came into the house holding the receiver in his tail above his back.

"Who was it?" Joey said.

"It was Mo. He's quite a card, with his phony 'I'm a Hollywood movie producer, I'll send my guy over' voice. I invited the raccoons around later for a garbage buffet, hope that's all right?"

"Sure, but you can have dinner with us, you know," Joey said.

"I appreciate that, Joey. It's just that I've come to enjoy being more of an animal. At least a bit."

It was midafternoon, and quite a crowd of Joey's mom's friends from work had come over. They were all joking and telling work stories.

"Hey, baby. Come here. I want you to meet these good people," his mother said from the living room. Joey laced his way through the grown-ups.

The doorbell rang.

"I'll get it," Joey said, relieved at his momentary escape.

A man in a suit holding a briefcase stood on the other side of the screen door. He looked too well dressed to be a cop, even a plainclothes one.

Joey popped his head back in the living room. "Mom? I think you better get this."

"May I help you?" Ann said, Joey next to her.

The man extended a business card. "Hi. I'm Victor Lapling. I represent Rick Darning. I believe you're expecting me."

Ann looked at Joey, who shrugged. "I'm sorry, sir. I don't know what this is about."

"I'm here for a Mr. Oswald Opossum. Rick called him earlier about making a movie. We were told to come over. I've got the contract right here. We'd like to fly him out tonight, if possible. You know what Hollywood's like. You got to get in there first with a good story like this," Mr. Lapling said.

Ann looked at Joey again.

"Oswald got a call this morning. He thought it was one of the raccoons joking around," Joey said.

"Dang," was all Ann said. She held the door open. "Please, Mr. Lapling, do come in. My son will get Oswald for you."

Joey returned with the possum scurrying at his feet, talking a mile a minute about Mr. Lapling being "for real" and how this could be Oswald's "big break after all!"

"I'm sorry, sir. The boy is a bit excitable," Oswald said, extending a paw. "I understand you want to speak with me? Do you understand Animal?"

Mr. Lapling gave Oz's paw a quick shake. "Yes, I do, as a matter of fact." He smiled, and held out a sheaf of papers to Oswald. "We've got the contract right here for your consideration. We were hoping you could fly out tonight, to Hollywood, so we can start filming your biopic tomorrow."

"Fly out? To Hollywood?" Oswald asked. The man seemed to be talking, but Oswald didn't hear what he was saying. Instead, everything that had happened in the last few weeks played out in his head: his attempts at getting in the newspaper, all that went wrong, the amazing beings he'd met and all the things they did together. He'd forgotten all about his prior aims at fame—hadn't even wished for it anymore. Then his eyes were drawn to the pen being waved in front of him.

"Mr. Oswald, do you want to sign? Are you all right?" Mr. Lapling said.

Oswald smiled as he took the pen with his back foot. "So sorry for my lapse. Just a little stunned is all—I never expected this!"

44

SOMETHING COOL

"Have fun. Don't forget—dinner's at five thirty," Miss Ann said.

Joey and Ghalib pedaled hard, east on Perry Street. They turned up Thirty-Third, leaned into the turn onto Bunker Hill, and generally tore around, up, down, and across the streets of Mount Rainier. Joey grinned. Silent except for the whir-whoosh of tires grabbing road. They pedaled in unison, free and powerful. Joey felt like he could do this forever and go anywhere.

Ghalib stopped at the corner ahead of Joey. "Want to see something cool?"

Joey stopped hard, inches from his friend. "Sure."

"Follow me."

They zoomed east on Bunker Hill, stopped before crossing Thirty-Fourth, then went right on Thirty-Fifth. Ghalib slowed and turned right onto a drive between the last two houses. He walked his bike to a gate, looked around, opened it, and darted in. Joey followed. The fence had signs all over it: *DO NOT ENTER,* and *DANGER—DEMOLITION SITE.*

This *was* cool.

Ghalib ditched his bike in some overgrown bushes. Joey did the same.

It was an old house, three stories tall. The first-floor windows were sealed up with sheets of metal. Ghalib walked up to a tree at the back of the house.

"You climb up onto that small roof, and then into the window. It's open."

"You sure?"

"Yeah—I've done it loads of times."

Ghalib climbed up the tree as though it were a ladder. He stepped onto the small roof, crouched down, and extended his hand. "Come on."

Joey jumped and grabbed the first branch, thick and strong with smooth bark. He swung his legs over the branch and climbed up to the roof.

Ghalib opened the window and slipped in. Joey's feet landed with an echo on the wooden floor. The house smelled musty and dusty.

The room they entered was empty except for a broken wooden chair and forgotten wire hangers in the closet. There wasn't a door on the closet, or in any of the rooms. There was a boarded-up fireplace.

"Come on. Let me show you something," Ghalib said.

They walked into a hallway and up the stairs to the third floor, the attic. Up there were old car tires, a garden hose, empty bottles and cans, a few hubcaps, and other stuff Joey couldn't make out in the dim light.

"Wow. Where did you get all this stuff?"

"It was already in the house mostly. Some of it was downstairs."

"Oh," was all Joey could think to say.

"Watch this," Ghalib said. He took one of the car tires and released it at the top of the stairs. The boys watched as it bounce-rolled down the stairs and down the hall.

"If you do it just right, it'll bounce off the wall, then go down the other stairs. You go down and watch."

Joey went down to the second floor and located the stairs to the first floor. Most of the steps were missing or rotted out.

"But how do we get the tires back after they go all the way down?" Joey called up to his friend.

"Don't worry about that," Ghalib called from the attic. As promised, a car tire bumped down from the attic, wobbled through the hall, and then dove down the skeletal steps to the ground floor. It smashed bits of the rotting wood on its way down. It was a satisfying sound.

"Wow. That's pretty cool," Joey said.

Another tire made the trip. Joey helped it along, giving it a push.

Ghalib appeared next to him, looked down at the tires at the bottom and grinned.

"Now for the fun part."

"What?"

"I'll show you."

Ghalib balanced on the diagonal piece of wood stretching from the first to second floors—the one that used to hold the steps. That was pretty much all that was left of the stairs. He turned around.

"There's a chair down here. I'll stand on that, you lie on your stomach, and I'll pass the tires up to you—"

But that was all he got to say. The wood collapsed under him. He slammed onto the floor beneath.

"Ghalib! Are you all right?"

He lay there, quiet. After a few seconds he got to his knees and gasped. "Wind knocked out of me—that's all."

"Oh my god, we've got to get you out of there. You OK? Anything broken?" Joey said.

"Nah, I'm OK. For real."

They both were quiet, staring at the last of the staircase lying on the floor.

"Is there anything down there like a ladder?" Joey said.

"I'll look."

Ghalib disappeared into the darkened first floor. He returned with a chair and a broom. "This is it."

"OK, I'll go outside and see if I can get one of those things off a window, get you out that way."

Joey climbed out the window and down the tree. The metal plates were screwed onto the house with those special screws you can't undo. He tried telling Ghalib through the boarded-up windows but it was no use. He looked around the yard for anything that might help. He found an old clothesline and climbed back in.

"It's no use. You can't get the screws out of the metal panels even with a screwdriver. Here." Joey threw one end of the rope down. "I'll tie it to something then you climb up."

"OK."

Joey tied his end of the rope to a radiator, tested the knots, and made a few extra. There was plenty of extra rope.

"Ready."

Ghalib tried, but the plastic covered rope was too thin and slippery.

"I'll tie it around me, then you pull me up." But with Ghalib a good twenty pounds heavier than Joey, there was no way.

"What about that hose in the attic? Maybe I could climb up that?"

Joey ran and got it, but it was rotten and crumbled when he lifted it.

"We need a ladder. Maybe I should go back home get Mr. Edwards. He has one—lives next door," Joey said.

"Won't he tell your mom?"

"I guess. But it's better than staying there forever."

They thought a minute.

"Maybe I could make loops in the rope and use them to climb up, like a rope ladder," Ghalib said.

But the loops tightened around his feet, and he couldn't get them back out.

"What about tying pieces of the wood down there into the rope, and step on those?" Joey said.

"Good idea." Ghalib tried it but the wood was too rotten.

"Wait there. I'll go get some sticks," Joey said.

"Yeah, I'll wait here."

"Right. Sorry."

Joey made another foray outside and returned with a bunch of sticks of different sizes.

After considerable trial and error, they got enough sticks that were strong enough tied into the rope at decent intervals. Joey worked from the top down, and Ghalib from the bottom up.

Joey tied the extra rope from the radiator to himself, braced his foot against the wall, and helped Ghalib up once he was close. They both lay panting.

"What time is it?" Joey said.

Ghalib checked his phone. "Almost six."

"Oh no. My mom's going to kill me," Joey said.

45

WE ARE FAMILY

Joey sped home, skidding to a stop in front of his house. His mom was on the porch. She looked mad.

"Sorry, Mom." He wheeled his bike inside the gate and closed it gently.

"'Sorry Mom'? You're forty-five minutes late, dinner's ruined, and I was *worried*. All I get is a 'sorry Mom'?" Her arms were crossed, and she tapped her foot. She looked taller than usual.

Joey hung his head. He didn't know what to say. He looked around, anywhere but her angry eyes. The water in Naja's pool rippled in the breeze. He hated that—it always made him think, for a second, she was there.

"When are we going to take that pool down?" he said.

His mother threw her arms in the air, shook her head, and walked back into the house. She was saying something, but Joey figured it was just as well he couldn't hear it. He wheeled his bike across the yard to the garage.

He dragged his feet back to the house, thinking about what to tell his mother about why he was late.

"Hi, Joey!" Naja said.

There she was, on the grass, preening her feathers still wet from a paddle in the pool.

Joey ran to her. "Naja! You're back!" He hugged the goose, and she laid her neck across his shoulder and honked.

"What in the world?" Ann came out on the deck and leaned on the railing.

"It's Naja—she's back!" Joey yelled.

Miss Ann didn't forget she was mad at Joey. Twenty-four hours without the Internet was his punishment. But it was hard for her to stay mad once she set eyes on Naja. They had a family dinner on the deck, Ann, Joey, Melvin, and Naja.

"So where did you go? Why did you fly off like that?" Joey asked. He still felt hurt over it.

"I went to find a flock, but then I realized I already had one," Naja said.

After dinner, Mr. and Mrs. Edwards and Zola joined them. Mrs. Edwards had made another cake, chocolate with buttercream icing this time.

"Cats don't like sweet things, but I'd love some of that buttercream icing, if that's OK," Melvin said.

"Of course it is," Ann said. She scraped a big spoonful off the cake and into his dish. Ann understood most of what Melvin said now.

They laughed, ate too much cake, and told stories until no one could keep their eyes open.

"Welcome back, Naja," Mrs. Edwards said. Everyone cheered, whistled, meowed, honked, or barked.

It was about two in the morning when Oswald's plane landed at Baltimore-Washington International Airport. He'd negotiated with the movie studio, and they agreed he could break his contract. The action-double possum gladly stepped into the

lead role for about half Oswald's fee. Oswald preferred to fly back home economy rather than first class, saving them more money, too. He wanted to be treated like a regular being.

He was the last stop for the SuperShuttle driver. Oswald had to wait an extra hour until one who spoke Animal was available—there weren't many. They motored south on the Baltimore-Washington Parkway. The trees were thick and green on both sides of the empty road. It smelled wonderful, much nicer than dry Los Angeles, at least for him.

"Mount Rainier, right?" The driver made eye contact through the rearview mirror.

"Yes, please. It's 3802 Thirty-Second Street."

The driver looked at him again. "Hey, you're not that famous possum I read about, are you? The one who made the video that got that lady out of jail?"

"No, that's not me. There's quite a few possums in Mount Rainier."

"It's a wild story. It made the cover of *People* magazine." He reached into the side pocket of his door, retrieved the magazine, and held it out for Oswald, who was on the seat right behind him.

"Take a look. It's pretty interesting. First possum to make a video, as far as they know."

The driver put his turn signal on. They went right. Oswald looked at the magazine cover—a photo of a random possum, not him. Melvin had warned him about this happening.

The driver chatted on, but Oswald only half-listened. He was thinking about Joey, and Melvin and Miss Ann and everyone else. He was thinking about the movies he wanted to watch with Joey, the things he wanted to do with Melvin, and the things he wanted to ask Zola and—

"Do you want help with your bags?" the driver said. They turned onto Thirty-Second Street.

"No, thank you. I'll be fine."

Oswald waited for the SuperShuttle to start off. He walked down Thirty-Second Street to Perry Street and turned right toward home. He thought it was better to give a fake address, in case his real one was in the papers.

He rolled his bag behind him holding the handle with his tail. The little wheels caught on the uneven sidewalk. No one was out. The front porches were empty. He passed one house cat he didn't know. He walked past the house where the roofers had been working, past the Edwardses' house, to Ann and Joey's front gate. The lights were out, but it looked warm inside.